LIVE

to

TELL

Debby Kruszewski

ISBN 978-1-64458-388-3 (paperback)
ISBN 978-1-64458-389-0 (digital)

Christian Faith Publishing, Inc.
832 Park Avenue
Meadville, PA 16335
www.christianfaithpublishing.com

Printed in the United States of America

How will they hear.
When will they learn.
How will they know?

— *Live to Tell*, Madonna

I entered our home and was startled by the door slamming behind me. I forgot that it still did that. You don't notice the noises when you are distracted by the people around you. Silence is scary. It is eerie.

The house was empty. I thought I had it all figured out. I thought I was in a good place with what had happened, what I had discovered within myself. I wasn't. I didn't even scratch the surface yet. I looked around the room as I had the island of the kitchen behind me. I didn't even recognize our home anymore. There are so many things I never saw. It was raw now that there was no one in it but me. The pictures on the refrigerator from Marisol and Pri stood there. Pictures of our family hung on the wall, slightly crooked. I can't remember ever spending the time to look at them and cherish them. I was busy living in it. Now it is a memory. *Dylan, I didn't realize how much I missed you.*

The creeks from the floorboards sang a harmonious song that I never heard of before. There was no TV playing in the background. No singing in the shower. No patter of feet running from room to room. It was just me alone in my house without my husband. I wore a new title—Mrs. Valerie Zavala—a widow. I was a widow. I didn't know what came with that title. *Is there a class? Do I need a certification? How do I tell people, "I'm sorry, Dylan will not be coming, because he is dead. My husband is dead." How will I handle the mail that still comes in his name?*

Bank of America: Attn: Mr. Dylan Zavala your balance is…

Cable: Attn: Mr. Dylan Zavala, would you like to continue your subscription for HBO?

Walgreens: Hello, this message is for Dylan Zavala. Your prescription is ready for pick-up.

Do I send out a tweet? "#dylanisdead hey y'all, my husband died on our wedding night. Please send wine. Thanks."

Or do I let the silence tell the story? I don't know how to do this. The downtime is a drug that I never took before. The hallucinations, the withdrawal, the night sweats. The flashbacks. It is evil, and I can't get enough. Right now, that is where I live—in the drug of missing Dylan.

I wore his watch. He never stopped wearing his big fancy Rolex that he bought when we lived in Manhattan. The glistening platinum body with a black face. It made him feel important. It gave him power. I can still feel the heat from him on my wrist. I can't take it off. When I remembered I had it on me, I brought it to my chest, whispering, "Dylan, Dylan, Dylan;" until it faded away. It came back again at some point during that hour. Then there was the silence again. It was so loud. I was in his closet and took everything off the hangers; everything out of the drawers and laid in the pile of Dylan's clothes. His socks on my face. His boxers on my tush. His favorite red, white, and blue flannel draper across my chest. I hugged it and smelled it until the feeling was numbing. All of this in the silence that danced in my brain when Dylan wasn't occupying the space. "Dylan, Dylan, Dylan," I repeated. The hour must be almost up. *What will I do for the rest of the hours I have left? I don't know what to do with myself.* I listened to the silence. The creaks from the floorboards. I listened for Dylan.

I moved myself into the bed and sank my face into his pillow. I could smell his sweat. I could smell the occasional cigarette he took after he told me he quit. Some of his salt and pepper hairs waited for him to return. *He's not coming home. It is my bed now.* This queen-sized proportion of cotton belonged only to me.

"Mrs. Zavala, which side would you prefer? We have both the left and the right available. We just had a sudden cancelation."

"I don't care," I answered. Because I didn't care anymore. I didn't have Dylan; it didn't matter.

I drifted into a sleep until my brain woke me up and asked me about Dylan. "Wait, don't you miss Dylan? How can you sleep?"

Then I was back up again. I took the watch to my chest and repeated his name repeatedly until I let the silence try to tell me something. I slumped back into the bed, face buried back in the pillow, and hoped to drift back asleep. I tried to place my body in the exact position he did when he slept like this. When he was mad. When he was ashamed. When he wanted to hide from me. When he wanted to be with me and didn't know how. When he missed Lydia. When he missed Olivia. When he didn't know how to express himself. When he was scared. When he was lonely. He slept with his head in this pillow. I wanted to feel his power. I wanted to take away his pain.

"Dylan, I want you back here with me," I said. The silence gave me the answer. I waited for the hour to be up and held my wrist to my chest. "Dylan, Dylan, Dylan." And I drifted away.

The door slammed and startled me, but not enough to take my head out of the pillow. "Valerie? Valerie? Hello! You haven't left this house in three days. Checking to see if you are still alive."

It was Frannie, Dylan's mother. She walked around the house and found me with my face in the pillow and the clothes all over the room. She came into the bed and laid next to me. She got into my ear. "I brought tequila," she said as she rubbed my hair; and when I didn't react, she smacked my ass.

I reached out my hand to take the bottle, pushed myself up to take a long swig, and went back into the pillow.

"Get up, just sit up for a bit with me," she said to me with a nudge.

I pushed myself around, and with my hair in my face, I took the bottle and downed a bit more. It felt good as it burned down my throat.

"This is that hard part. Right now," she said as if it was an approval to drink more.

I couldn't cry as I was beyond that emotion. I was in the "drink tequila in mass quantities" phase. Frannie was mourning herself, and I didn't know how to console her. We sat in my bed, leaning on each other, and drank Dylan's secret stash of "this is good shit, y'all." It was saved for special occasions, like this one. The owner of this bottle who was no longer here to drink it. *Cheers to you, Dylan, I can't let go of you.*

We emptied the bottle and fell asleep into each other, and when my brain reminded me, "Hey girl? What about Dylan?" I opened my eyes and looked around for him. Then he was there by the window, looking out at the early morning sky. He was shirtless and concentrated on the silence, drinking coffee, still wearing his favorite hat. He didn't look over. "I miss you too, Valerie, I really do."

I cried. I finally cried and watched him. He took deep breaths.

"I love you so much, Dylan, I love you, I miss you! I need you. Dylan, I can't live without you."

His tears started to run down his face. "*Mi amor*, oh, *mi amor*. I love you. I am not ready to leave you. But I have to go."

I went up behind him and found my perch in between his shoulder blades. I placed my hands right above his underwear line. This was us. This was my comfort zone. I could smell him. I felt him. We had our proper goodbye. We stood in the silence. The wind called as it picked up. "Oh, Ms. Valerie, you were everything to me. I promise to watch over you and the family. Please go and have a life. Please. I will always be waiting for you, *mi amor*. Always." He hugged my hands on his body and kissed my forehead.

"Ms. Valerie, enjoy your day. I am going to escort Dylan from here," Peter said; and then they were gone.

I held my hand out to see if I could still feel him, but all I felt was air. They were gone.

"I saw it," Sofia said from the doorway of my bedroom.

"I did too," Frannie said from the bed. Pri came over and gave me a hug from behind.

"I am so glad that Dylan came to visit you. You were too sad," she said and hugged me tighter.

I was touched by an angel. My angel. My husband. We all looked at each other in astonishment and disbelief of what just happened. But it happened. It happened to me.

"Okay, ummm… yeah," I said and brushed my hand through my hair. I held my bottom lip. All just the same as Dylan would have done in that moment. "He will always be within me," I added and they all shook their heads in acknowledgement.

We organized his clothes and gave some to John, took what we wanted, made piles for friends and family—the rest we gave to charity. I kept his favorite flannel and a few hats and a few other items that I could not part with. He was parting from our lives; now my closet was all mine and half-empty.

The girls were all excited that Marisol was coming home from spending a few weeks with her biological father.

"Can I make Marisol a sign?" Pri asked me as we were getting ready to meet her at the airport.

"Absolutely, love! She will be so excited. Thank you, Pri," I said and kissed her head. She was in her mid-twenties and still the same little girl I met when I first arrived in Texas. Her learning disabilities got better, but she never really grew up as a woman. She was content as the little girl she wanted to be with Bingo and her Barbies. She loved animals and worked on the farm. She lived in Frannie's house as Frannie wanted the companionship. She was so happy in her own world. She was never fazed by any anger in her life. She was a true vision of what God wants for us all—to be content with his love in her heart. As I am learning to love myself, Pri is one of my greatest professors.

We stood at baggage claim and waited for Marisol to exit the plane. Pri held her sign, and as she saw us, she ran to us and hugged as many of us as she could at the same time. I missed my girl so much. We got into the car, and as the engine turned on, Pri turned to Marisol.

"Dylan came to visit Valerie." No one knew what to say.

"He did? That is wonderful!" Marisol said. I smiled as it was a happy occasion.

"We all must learn to love life and live it to the fullest. That is what Dylan wants for us," I said to the car as I drove into our sea of green at the farm.

"Amen to that," Frannie said. She was a tough cookie. This was hard; to watch all the men in her life disappear out of their stupid arrogance. I don't know how she did it.

I helped Marisol carry her bags into the house where she ran right up the stairs to her room. I followed behind her. I was so happy to not have to live in this house alone anymore. I watched her go through her things and start to unpack. She grew up so much from this trip, this experience. "So, I hope that you had fun on your visit. This has been a lot for you," I said to her as she was preoccupied in her stuff.

"Yes, it is a lot. But it was nice. We had a nice visit. I spent a lot of time with Madison. She is so cool, Mom. I am excited to have a cool sister. I love Pri, and I don't know Olivia. John is away. It is nice to get to know someone that is so like me. It was awesome. She has fancy clothes, drives a fancy car, like you. Christopher is laid back. I have been told that is not really who he used to be. The accident must have really set him back. He is kind of slow and always in pain. It is sad. But he was kind and we had fun. This is so weird, but I do have a connection to him."

I sat on her bed as I listened to her. She was better at processing this then I was. I sat and listened. Marisol came to sit with me on the bed. It felt like *Gilmore Girls*, both of us in a team together, no men in our life around; daddy issues, a total scene for their next Netflix show. She matured so much these past few weeks, I wanted to soak her in. She played with my hair. She missed me too.

"So how are you? I was worried about you," she asked in concern.

I kept my distance when she was on this trip. I didn't want her to know how sad I was. I didn't want to ruin her bond with Christopher. "I am glad that you are home, sweetheart," I said with some reassurance.

"I can see that you are sad."

"I am sad. I miss him so much. It hurts, it really hurts. But this is just a season. I will get through this. We will get through this as a family. You are here now. School will start up soon. I will find a way to be distracted. We all must continue moving forward and get back into our lives. That is what Dylan wants for us. This is the hard part. But I know he is with me."

"Me too. I miss him so much." She moved over to hug as we laid in her bed. No tears. They were not necessary now.

"I have something for you." I went into my room and brought out a bag with a few of Dylan's things that I saved for her.

"What is this?" she asked.

"It's a bunch of things I saved for you that I am sure you wanted to keep from Dylan. He loved you so much, Marisol. I hope that you know that."

"I do. I love him too. He will always be my dad. Christopher will always be Christopher. I just don't know what that means to me right now."

"Understood."

She went through the bag and held each item to her chest, closing her eyes and soaking in each piece. It was a few shirts, a few hats, his boots that she wore to make fun of him years ago. I gave her his cross that he wore. She always played with it when she rested on his chest to fall asleep. She put it on and I don't think she has taken it off.

"Mom, whatever happened between you and Christopher? Why did you choose Dylan over him?"

"Okay, wow, that is a loaded question. But yes, you deserve an answer. It is complicated and it's not. I somehow knew Christopher or thought I did from a previous life. I really did. I had pictures of him in my head, I had conversations with him in my sleep. He was a consumption of my mind. It was horrible. And yes, he was not such a nice person. When we found each other, he belonged to someone else. I belonged to Dylan. It just wasn't meant to be." I stopped there as I felt so vulnerable and mad at myself for the dumb mistakes I had made. I did have an affair and cheated on Dylan. But it brought us the child we couldn't conceive. As I was telling her this story, did I do what was right for our family? Or was it out of selfishness?

"He told me about when you went to see him in the hospital."

"Yes, I did."

"Why?" she asked, and then there was a long pause. It hurt to be asked the question when it was a secret for so long. I started to cry and moved myself out of the room. Marisol followed as she put on one of Dylan's flannels. I went to grab for mine and did the same.

"I was weak and I couldn't resist him. It was foolish. I hurt Dylan, and he didn't know until his death. He had hurt me too. But if I didn't make this foolish mistake, we wouldn't have had you. We needed a baby. We were drowning from our loss of our first child. It was hard to get over that. I don't know that we ever got over that."

"You had another baby? What?" she said, upset. *Oh, the secrets we kept! I forgot them and now I am not sure I know of their truths.*

"I had a miscarriage. In Mexico. It's a long story, Marisol. I am not ready to go back there and talk about it.

"Mom! Why don't I know this?"

"It is not for you to know. I am telling you because your father has passed and I don't know. Marisol, I am not perfect, and I am working on that. Please, just please let it be." I stood at the window with my wrist to my chest and chanted to Dylan in my head. I wanted him to come back to me and give me a hug. *Come and interrupt an argument between Marisol and I.* He was no longer here to do that for us. *Oh, Dylan, I miss you so much.*

"Fine," she said with anger and went into her room, slammed the door, and turned the volume up on her speakers as loud as it could go. The pictures on the wall danced to the beat. My glass jar from Sheila's bedroom sat on my dresser and danced its way to the floor and shattered into a thousand pieces. I felt like a horrible mother and wasn't getting fired anytime soon. I let the hour pass and went back into burying my face into Dylan's pillow and let the noise numb my pain.

"*What is going on in here?*" Frannie came barreling into the house and up the stairs into Marisol's room and turned off the music. "What is wrong with you?" she demanded from Marisol who stood in disbelief that Frannie was not afraid to barge into her room without permission.

"I am just mad and want to listen to music and not listen to *her!*" She pointed at my room and I did not take my face out of the pillow.

"That is your mother and you will respect her, young lady."

"I will not. Her secrets and lies. She killed my dad and ruined Christopher's life, and now she is ruining mine." Her tone turned into anger so quickly. *I guess this is how she really feels, and she is not wrong.*

Frannie took her by the arm and dragged her into my bedroom and shoved her into the bed with me. I did my best not to move.

"Get up!" Frannie said to me as she pulled me by my hair and was not waiting for me to do it myself. We sat in the bed, all together draped in Dylan's clothes with tears and anger. I was so weak. I couldn't react.

"So tell her, Marisol. Tell your mother what you just told me. How her lies hurt you, go on…"

Marisol did not look at me, and I just looked into the wall with a sigh because I felt like I was hurt so much already. I was numb. My daughter deciding I was a criminal could not really wound me as much as I thought. But it hurt, and she was right. I deserved the pain.

"*No!*" she screamed and tried to go back into her room.

"Do it!" Frannie said with a strong hold on her shoulders. "Do it now!" she demanded again.

Marisol screamed out of frustration, and when she was done, I turned to her and looked her in the eyes. "Yes, Marisol. Please, please tell me. Tell me what you need to say and say it to my face. I made choices that I am not proud of. But I made them for the good of my family. I gave you a wonderful life with Dylan as your father. Why don't you ask your new favorite sister, Madison, how wonderful it was to have Christopher as a dad? Did you have that conversation with her? Or were you too busy driving around in her fancy car and wearing her fancy jewelry? Is that what you see as a wonderful life? Stuff? Because if that is what you want, you can have it. Anything, because her fancy things are the pain she has from her father not being there for her when she was growing up. Did she tell you that part?

"I think you have a pretty nice deal here, Marisol. Your father, Dylan, *loved* you. He *loved* you! You have a brother and a sister that spent time with you and were always good to you and they *love* you. Did you know that I had a sister? Did you know what she was to me? No, you don't. Do you know that I have a brother, Marisol? Do you? Yeah, I do, his name is Todd. Where is he? Yeah, I don't know either. How many kids does he have? I don't know. Do you know? Do you know why, Marisol, do you? Because if you wanted the childhood that I had, then you should have had Christopher as your father. Then all the stuff that Madison has and lives with could be yours too. I could buy you all that shit if that is want you really want. Is that what you want, Marisol?

"You have a chance to have a new relationship with your father. He wants to start over with his kids with the time he has left here on Earth. Because he doesn't have much time left. Did he tell you that? Did he mention that he has cancer and it is at stage four? Maybe that is why he is weak. Please keep reminding me how horrible I am to let you spend time with him before he is no longer with us.

"Marisol, you don't have any idea what it feels like for your mother to not love you and not do what is right for you. I did everything for you, Marisol, that my mother didn't. You were never left without love. You have a wonderful grandmother standing next to you. You never met my mother because she killed herself after she disowned me. I have very little things, Marisol, very little things from my childhood, and especially from my mother. I had *one* thing that I touched every day from her to remind me that I have a great life, and I don't want the life she had. *One thing*. It is now sitting shattered on the floor in front of you. You just broke it, so thank you for that, Marisol. Thank you so much. So now what is it that you have to say to me? Please, I really want to hear it."

Frannie let her grip go on Marisol's shoulders so she could react.

"I'm sorry, Mom, I am so sorry." She started to cry and tried to grab for me, but I pushed her off and stormed out of the room, down the stairs, out the door, and straight to the rose patch where Dylan and Peanut lived. I was so angry and felt so relieved at the same time. I went there and fell to my knees and grabbed dirt with strong fists to help with the pain.

"Dylan, do you hate me as much as I feel like you should?" I asked.

"No, *mi amor*. I love you. Be patient with her, this is a lot all at once. 'Just a season,' you always say. Listen to your heart, love, I am always with you."

Marisol attempted to run after me, but Frannie stopped her. "Let her go. She still needs time to heal. We all do." She hugged Marisol who was also upset and confused. "Let's go into town and see if we can pick out a new jar for your mom and maybe some flowers? Marisol, she did what was right for you. I hope that you understand she did it out of love."

"I know, I can see that now," Marisol replied. Frannie and Marisol got into the truck and left the farm to go seek out what they could find to replace my past with a happy future. They brought back a bouquet of red roses in a lovely vase that sat on the kitchen island for the next week.

"Daddy, I love you. Christopher could never replace you," Marisol said to Dylan one morning as she admired the roses and held onto the vase.

"I know, *mi amor*, I know. Be kind to your mother. She always did what was best for you."

When the flowers were past their prime, Marisol took them to have them crushed into rosary beads in honor of Dylan. The small bottom-based vase was a pink glass. She put it back on my dresser and filled it with the lonely pearls.

* * * * *

Dylan and Lydia moved into the vacant house across the street from Madeline and Cal. Peanut had a beautiful crib that was laced with gingham pink sheets, the same ones I bought for her when I found out I was pregnant. Lydia grabbed Dylan's arm to lead him to the master bedroom after he dropped Peanut into the crib for the evening. "I'm not ready yet," he said and went into the third bedroom and closed the door.

"I'm not ready either, Dylan. Not yet," I said to him, and he blew me a kiss goodnight.

*   *   *   *   *

School started, and before we knew it, the bonfires and homecoming dances were all that Marisol could talk about during her junior year in high school. For her birthday, I bought her the Audi convertible that she picked out. It perfectly suited her personality; she earned it and deserved it. She didn't wear much make-up; her beauty was more than enough. She had such a confidence, I was so jealous of it. She was a cheerleader and played on the tennis team. She had the good grades and already had her heart on going to a prestigious college. She had the boys wrapped around her finger, but she wasn't interested in a boyfriend. "Not now, I'm just having fun. No need to be so serious," she said. She was my sassy pants daughter, and I couldn't have been prouder.

The bonfire was always a good time. I was so glad I had one more kid still in school to enjoy the ceremonies. Marisol had her big cheerleading act at half-time and at the bonfire that evening. She was so excited. We all went and could not wait to watch her shine. As the clock ticked down the minutes to the end of the second quarter, I reached for my phone to FaceTime with Christopher.

FaceTime call:

"Hello, how are you?"

"All right, just getting my chemo treatment."

"Ouch, I am sorry. Marisol is just about to come out, so are you good? Do you want to watch it with me?"

"Oh, Valerie, that would be amazing."

"Great! Okay, turning the camera so you can watch. They are ready to start!"

I held the phone for him to watch. She did flips and jumps. She was in the basket tosses, and wow, I was nowhere near and daring as she was. When it was over, I turned the phone back to me and his smile was wide.

"Thank you, Valerie, this made my day."

"Good, so how are you doing? Are you okay?"

"I am getting there. Getting better each day. I can't believe I am still alive."

"I am glad that you are. God is good!"

"All the time. So when do I get to see you ladies again?"

"Yeah, we should take a trip. Let me talk to Marisol after the weekend and set a date. Goodnight, Christopher."

We watched the rest of the game. Our team won. We set the bonfire into flames, and I watched Marisol smile and be the center of attention to all the cute football players that all tried so hard. I thought of Taylor and how handsome he was and how special he made me feel when we were a couple in high school. Then when he made me look and feel like a fool in college. What would have happened if I did sleep with him in high school? Would I have ever met Christopher? Would I have ever met Dylan? *Oh, Dylan, how much I miss you. Marisol is so much a product of you. I see you when she is in this glory. She says, "Y'all" and slaps her leg when she laughs, just like you would. She brushes her fingers through her hair, just like you. She wears your hat everywhere she goes. Even though you didn't make her, you molded her. I did it for us, Dylan. I did it for you. But now, we don't have you, Dylan. It still really hurts.*

She wore a tight pink dress with big heels that she was still learning to master walking in. We had practiced the past few weeks walking a pretend catwalk at night, up and down the kitchen to the living room, the hallway upstairs, walking down the stairs. She still stumbled. "Mom, how do you walk so good in heels? This is hard, y'all."

"Ha-ha, well, I always wore heels. Your dad was tall, so I wanted to be as close to him as possible," I said in a dreamy fashion, remembering when we lived in the city, when we came home from work, and ate dinner on our small kitchen island. Sometimes, I sat in his lap and cuddled into his neck as he finished his blueberry pie. I drank from his glass of wine and hoped that he didn't notice. He chuckled. He rubbed my side and when he finished his pie and I finished his wine, we went into the bedroom.

"Mom, hello? Did I lose you?" she said as I was living in that fantasy. "So, Marisol, who is escorting you to the dance tonight?"

"Michael."

"Which one is Michael?"

"Mom! Michael is the guy from the math team. He is super cute."

I dreamed of Christopher when I was her age. She dreamed of nerds. She had so many choices of who she could be with. Her confidence was so strong. Mine was so fixated on one man. How I wish I had her trust in myself. Trust in God. *Oh, how different we are.*

Michael drove up in a truck, and his nerdy body came out in a tux with a corsage. He did have a nice smile. He was kind. He so admired Marisol. She knew it. They said their goodbyes, we took pictures, and then they were off.

They went to the dance. It was in the school gym decorated this year as the "Land of the Sea." Michael and Marisol danced to each slow song. He held her waist kept at a perfect distance. She held her arms around his neck. They smiled at each other. Drops of sweat formed on his forehead. He was so nervous. When no one was looking, their friends spiked the punch, and before the girls became too giggly and noticeably not able to walk in their heels, they left the prom.

Their crew went out to a field and drank beers, created a mixed drink consisting of any other liquors they could find with juices and sodas. I am sure it was something horrible. They danced to the car radio. Some girls lost their virginity that night. Some boys did too. Some girls regretted it. Some didn't. The boys were scared out of their mind of it.

Marisol laid in the bed of the truck with Michael and gazed at the stars. She held her head over his arm, and he didn't pressure her or push for anything further than that. They gazed at the stars and listened to the crowd behind them. When morning came, they all went out for breakfast and laughed at the night they had. Michael drove Marisol home and walked her to the door. She kissed him on the porch and grazed her fingers down his body, just to give him enough to hold him over until they were both ready. "Thank you, Michael, I am so glad I went with you to the prom. It was so special to me," she said as she pressed her lips into his and pushed her hands on his chest.

"Marisol, I am the luckiest guy in the world right now. Thank you for letting me take you. This is a dream come true." He held onto her elbows and as red as his face was, the sweaty palms and shaking knees, he gave her a kiss back. They both knew that this was not going to end right here.

She came into the house late in the morning. I was trying to pretend I was not up worrying. Frannie and I sat at the island over our morning breakfast meeting. Marisol danced her way around the room, grabbed a piece of bacon, and hummed a tune in her head as she dazzled up the stairs into her room.

"So I guess she made it through the night alive?" Frannie said. I laughed and wanted to be as cool as possible, but the Gilmore girl in me ran up the stairs to find her laying in her bed, sprawled out with the same smirk on her face as when she walked in.

"Oh hey, Marisol, what's up? Like, yeah, how was the prom, yo?" I said in my lame mom voice.

"Am I being a good Gilmore girl?" she giggled and sighed.

I was afraid she lost her virginity, but she didn't.

"Mom, he is so dreamy."

"That kid that picked you up? Yeah? He looks like a nerd. I guess you like nerds? Why a nerd over all the adorable football players?" I asked.

"Mom, he is so cute. He looks at me so nervous. He always asks to take me out. He never gives up. He doesn't try to impress me. He just looks at me with stars in his eyes and never gives up. He didn't try anything on me when all the jerk football players do. They are so immature. Michael, he is just sweet, and his kiss was everything. Mom, I really do like him."

She spoke in a dreamy fashion. I wish I had something to compare it to when I was her age.

"So, Mom, how do you know?"

"Know what, *mi amor*?" I asked.

"How do you know when it is love? How do you know when it will be forever? I guess I am still confused about you. I know that you loved Dylan, there is no doubt about that. But what about Christopher? When did you know that you loved him? Why? How? He told me how he knew how he fell in love with you. I don't know your side. I am just confused. Can you love more than one? Does that ruin the fairytale?" The question was clearly Gilmore girl maturity for the mother and daughter conversation. *Can I be as strong and witty as Loreli is?*

"First of all, there is no fairy tale. It just feels like one when you get all tingly for someone. I learned too late in life that you can't love someone until you love yourself. Your grandfather told me that when I was in my hospital bed just as Dylan died. Oh, I had a desire for Christopher and didn't understand why. I let it control me. I let it ruin me. I let it make me do stupid things. I didn't listen to what God's plan was and let him lead the way. I did what I told God I wanted and let that lead the way. It led me in bad directions.

"I believe that God has a master plan. We need to listen to it. So listen to yours. Let God tell you what is in your heart and believe in it. I already know that you love and respect yourself. You are a very special girl. Dylan would be so proud of you. So as I said, let God lead the way. You will make mistakes. God will take you back to where you need to be. He has a plan for me, he has a plan for you. I believe that Dylan was my gift. I am so grateful for how everything turned out in our lives. He was my true love. No one can take that away. I met him and our feeling toward each other was so strong. Nothing could tear us apart. He is still in my heart."

"What would have happened if it was the other way around? If Dylan was your Christopher and Christopher was your Dylan?" she asked. *She watches to much* Awkward.

"I don't know. All I know is that I followed a path. The journey that God led me on. It is not the destination. It is the path you chose along the way. Stay on your path. Follow your heart." I smiled as she had wise questions to ask.

"Do you love Christopher? Did you love him when you were with Dylan? Why didn't it work out? Why didn't you tell anyone that he is my father?" *Another bold question.*

"I didn't know until the day Dylan died. I suspected through the years Dylan questioned things, but we both dismissed it. I was afraid when we ran into Christopher at the airport in Colorado that everyone knew. No one went in that direction out loud. I think in our heads we all thought it. I believe that is why Dylan beat Christopher up so badly and ran away. I don't believe he meant to take his life that night. He came to me in a dream telling me so. He wanted to stay and continue as your father. I know that he would have.

"When you guys volunteered to donate blood for Dylan and Christopher, you were a direct match for Christopher and no one else was. Right then, I knew. I held a secret that I wasn't sure about for years. I took a chance, but I did it for love. I can only believe I did the right thing. I love Dylan so much. I love our family so much. I didn't want to upset anything.

"So, Christopher. He had so many chances to come to me, and he didn't. He never broke up with his wife until his daughters were much older. He wasn't a nice person. He gave up on me. We would have been alone and miserable. I didn't want that for us. I didn't want to leave the other kids. I had so much love for everyone here. The decision was easy. I did have love for him and wanted to know what that meant. The consequences were horrible. I confessed so many times. I had to let him go to love Dylan and the family. I just did. I do hold love for him, but I was not in love with him. Sometimes I do wonder, but I am glad that I did what I did. That path led me to the family we needed to be. I will not look back or regret any of it. I hope you can understand that."

"Thank you, Mom, I do. I think if I didn't watch you and Dylan, I would have gone after a dumb football guy and had been lost and hurt, confused. Michael makes me feel so special, but I am so young. My heart wants him, but no offense, I don't want to get lost in one person so young and try to find it later on. I will follow my heart and hope it leads me back to him. I just want to see what else is out there before I do something I regret. I have faith."

"You are a smart faithful girl. It was fun tonight?"

"Oh, Mom, it was. I am so glad." Marisol was starting to pass out as she was up all night.

"Great, get some rest. We can talk later." I gave her a kiss and closed the door. *I am so grateful to have an amazing daughter.*

FaceTime call:

"Marisol."

"Hello, Christopher, how are you feeling?"

"Much better, thank you. Doing well. I am done with chemo and feeling good. So Marisol, your mother tells me that you are looking at colleges? Where are you thinking? I really would like to come with you on a visit."

"Well, I want to look at Texas A&M, Georgetown, Princeton, Villanova, and Duke. Mom wants to start looking next weekend."

"Wow, nice list, little lady. Start at Georgetown and you guys can come and stay here with me. How does that sound?"

"Okay, great! We will do that."

"Great, Marisol. I am so proud of you."

"Thank you, Christopher, that means a lot to me."

They hung up the phone and we booked reservations to head to DC and visit Georgetown University. Dylan loved college basketball. He loved for her to go to a school with a win under their belt. It made me believe he was with us.

We walked to campus on a sunny day in the fall where the leaves were of perfect fall colors and draped the campus greens. Marisol walked ahead of us and hung on each word the tour guide told her. She was in a college dream zone. We walked behind them and giggled at her excitement. Our feet kicked up leaves, and Christopher and I occasionally bumped into each other. Sometimes by accident, but mostly on purpose. I kept my arms wrapped around me as the air became cooler, and my sweater would, in the next few weeks, not be enough to keep me warm.

Marisol went with the group for the "student only" part of the tour. Christopher and I went to take a break on a bench. We sat in awkward silence until he put his hand on my knee and I put my head on his shoulder and reached to hold his hand. "I am so glad to be here with you, Valerie," he said. His tone had become so calm and relaxed. He was not the loud and aggressive man I met many years ago in a hotel bar.

"When were you going to tell us?" I asked boldly.

"I don't know, Valerie. I don't know."

"So how many days do you have left?"

"They told me that I may not make it to the end of the week three years ago, and I am still here. But I don't have much time left. I don't know."

"What do you want to do?"

"I want to spend every moment with you, Marisol, and Madison. It would mean the world to me to have my other daughter to come, but she no longer speaks to me. I just want to have the family I always wanted. Valerie, I have had you in my heart for so long. Why was I so foolish? Why did I do this to myself? To us? I didn't have a life until I had you in it. I don't have you in it, and now my life is almost over. It's so much to ask of you, but please, Valerie. I want nothing more than to have a life with you, the last moments. Can you give me the last days of my life? Please?"

He was vulnerable. He was weak. He needed me. I had to do this for him. "Yes."

"Valerie, you are so my dream I have always wanted. Thank you."

"Thank Jesus. He made this happen." I kissed his forehead and could not look at him as my emotions were all over the place. We decided to not tell Marisol just yet. *Just another secret she will find out at the wrong time and wrong moment. I am not perfect, y'all.*

We went back to Christopher's house and I made a fresh tomato sauce with pasta. We sat at the dinner table that overlooked the back-yard to his golf course community. We drank wine and let Marisol make us laugh with her fun stories of the day and the excitement to maybe enter into Georgetown University. Christopher and I stared at each other as she spoke.

After a few stories, she realized we were no longer listening to her anymore. She caught the vibe and knew there was something more going on in that room. She excused herself to the living room where she called her friends and sent out Instagram posts. Christopher and I finished our wine and retreated to the back porch to a small fire he built for us.

"This is all I ever wanted, Valerie. Kids, our kids. Sitting on the back porch with you by my side. Letting me admire your beauty and brush back your hair. This is what I wanted. I feel so complete."

I snuggled into his neck and closed my eyes as he held me close to him. We enjoyed the fire and each other.

* * * * *

Dylan walked outside of the house, frustrated and sad. He paced in front of the house, pretending to mow the lawn that was perfectly manicured. He did anything to waste the time away. Cal came outside as he saw Dylan frustrated and trying to fight it.

"This is so hard," Dylan said to Cal. Cal put his arm over him and they took a walk down the block.

"She needs to move on, Dylan. You know why she has to do this. It is all part of God's plan."

"I know she needs to continue her life. But I love her so much. I was not ready to let her go."

"Then why did you?" Cal said, and Dylan was confused as he didn't see that he did chose to leave.

"I am so foolish."

"No, you are not. Don't give up on her. As she says, 'Just a season.' You are in her heart. Not him. Remember that and believe that. She has *you* in her heart."

"Thank you. I will be strong and give her what she needs to continue her life. I will let her know that it is okay."

"Good. Now let's go back to my house. Madeline is going to grill up some steaks tonight. Bring over Peanut. We can share a few beers. You will get through this. We will go to visit the big man soon. He will show you that it will all be okay. Dylan, it will be okay." They smiled and walked back to the house. Dylan gathered the girls and they went over and cracked open some beers. He sat on the back porch with Peanut on his chest playing with his cross as he tried to get her to sleep.

"Thanks, y'all, for welcoming us to your family. I am blessed."

"Thank you for being here," Sheila said as she cheered right back to him.

* * * * *

That night, I slept in the guest bedroom with Marisol. I was awoken in the middle of the night by a loud noise outside. No one else was startled by this but me. I tiptoed out of the room and danced into the kitchen. Christopher and Marisol slept away.

I heard the swing on the back deck swing away in the middle of the night and saw a small twinkle of the fire left. I went outside and sat down. I felt my family around me. I felt a peace around me. I heard voices. I heard drinks being drunk. I heard laughs. I heard Dylan. I felt him. I sank into a body that wasn't there. But it was there. I brought my hand up to his chest where Peanut slept. He kissed my forehead and played with my hair.

"Valerie. I love you. Don't be afraid to have a life. Don't be afraid to move on. I love you, Ms. Valerie. I am here waiting for you. We are here waiting for you, *mi amor*. Now go and do what you need to do. Ask for me when you need me. Talk to me when you need to talk to me. Love me, but go and find what you need on Earth. Don't waste a moment. Don't stop being you."

"I never want to hurt you, Dylan. Never."

"You are not, my love. This is just a season. This is not our season. Now go."

I was pushed by a sudden jolt and then I was there alone. The fire had no more twinkle. Dust swirled around the yard, and after a few moments, I could smell Dylan again. A feather whisked by and I grabbed it. I knew what I needed to do. "Thank you Dylan. I love you too."

I went inside and tiptoed back into the house into Christopher's room and crawled into his bed behind him. He embraced my arm around his and smiled.

* * * * *

They all went to mass every day as that is what you do in heaven. They went as a family as neighbors and as brothers and sisters to God. Dylan carried Peanut, and Lydia walked beside them. They didn't talk much. She was still lost and she did not have the hold over Dylan that she once had. It upset her. They went through the motions. Their house was a family of two and a roommate. They walked to mass. She walked like a zombie.

"I know you still love her," she said to Dylan one day.

"I do still love her, Lydia. I am not going to apologize for that."

"You never loved me," she said.

"Lydia, that is not true. I loved you. We were so young. We were so stupid. You lied to me. You were never pregnant. That ruined me. You married my brother. Do you know how upsetting that was for me? I fell out of love with you, Lydia. You asked me to. You basically forced me to."

"I wanted it to be you, Dylan. I did. But I did fall in love with Miguel and messed that up."

"Lydia, you need to repent and get over this. You will never move on with your soul if you don't get over this. Miguel loved you. I don't know why, but he did. I recognized that and I walked away. Don't be mad at me for finding love. I had a woman in my head and it was Valerie. I needed to be with Valerie, and right now, this is not the easiest thing to go through. But I have to keep moving on."

As they entered into the church, a familiar face came over to sit by them. Dylan didn't look up as he was attending to Peanut.

"Hello, Dylan," Miguel said as he looked forward with his hands crossed.

"Miguel!" he said in excitement, and Lydia looked over.

"Hello, Lydia, you look beautiful as ever today," he said to her as he reached over to hug her, passing over Dylan. She smiled.

The mass began. Dylan moved over for them to sit together, and as the mass went on, Miguel felt bold enough to ask for her hand, and she accepted. She needed him today.

When mass was over, they walked back down to the house and Dylan invited Miguel over for coffee. They all connected at the table. Then Dylan went to take Peanut for a walk and give them time alone. Cal went outside to take the walk with Dylan.

"How are you doing?" Cal said.

"Better today. Each day gets a little better. I just found my brother and it feels good. I have my baby with me. We had time with the good Lord. God is good. Today is a good day."

"Good!" Cal said and slapped Dylan on the shoulder. They walked slow and admired the neighbors and beauty of the land around them. Dylan was slowly getting used to his surroundings. "We will go to meet the big man soon Dylan. Are you ready?"

"I hope so."

"He will let you know that all is okay. It will all be okay, Dylan."

"Thank you, Cal, I am so glad that I met you."

They walked back to the house, and when Dylan went inside, Miguel and Lydia sat anxiously on the couch for him to come home. They stood up holding hands as he entered.

"Hello, guys. Hope that you are having a nice visit. I will just be upstairs."

"Dylan, wait," Lydia said as it took her the whole afternoon to build up that courage. "We want to talk to you," she said.

"Ah, *si*," Dylan said and went to sit on the couch across from them with Peanut in his arms.

"Dylan, Lydia and I want to reconnect and get back together. This is so crazy. I want Lydia to come and live with me. I know it sounds like I am asking for permission, but I feel like I am. I also want to make amends with you. We were brothers. You did so much for me, the family, the farm. Look at what the farm became? It was all you, Dylan. I fell for Lydia and I didn't see it happening. I didn't ever mean to hurt you, but I did. I don't think I ever said I was sorry. Please accept my apology."

"Dylan, I am also sorry. I was so cruel to you. I hurt that precious baby in your arms. I took that precious baby away from her loving parents. I ask you for forgiveness. Can you ever forgive me?"

Dylan held his bottom lip with his left hand and sat back onto the couch as he brushed his other hand through his hair. He looked out the window to Sheila and Ashley dancing around the sprinkler across the street. "Valerie, what would you do? Would you forgive Sheila and Ashley if they asked you?"

"Dylan, my love. Yes, I would. Forgive, my love. Forgive," I said back to him. He took his focus back to the room.

"Ah *si, si*. Yes, I forgive you both. We must forgive to move on. Come and give me a hug."

They came over for a hug. Dylan brought Peanut to her crib. Lydia packed her things and Miguel escorted her to his house. Dylan stood on the porch and waved goodbye to them.

* * * * *

The weekend was over, and as we packed our things to head back to the airport, Christopher and I took Marisol to the couch to have a chat with her.

"Marisol."

"Yes, you guys are creeping me out. What is going on?"

"Marisol, so there is something that you need to know." I stood up and walked to the window as I had such a hard time to face her. Christopher sat up into his lap to hold himself up. I turned back around and sat with him, holding his hands as he needed it right now.

"So, Marisol, I am going to take you home, and then I am going to come right back. Christopher has entered into what is called hospice. Do you know what that means?" *Please answer yes as this is so hard to explain.*

"Kind of?"

"Okay, so this is when your cancer is no longer curable and they give you drugs to rest comfortably until you pass away. So he is getting set up tomorrow."

"What? I thought you were better? Why didn't you tell me?" Marisol stood up and came to our couch and held our hands as she rested on his side.

"Marisol, it all came aggressively and he did get better. But then it took a hard turn. It is up to you what you want to do. But if you don't want to come back with me, I think this may be your last good-bye to Christopher."

"OMG! Why? Why? No, Christopher, you can't die. You just can't!" As Marisol stood up to run away, I went to follow her and caught her just as she was about to head for the back door.

"Marisol, I need you to be strong. Please. He needs you. You came back into his life for a reason. Take advantage of it. My mom died and we were not even speaking. You have the chance to spend time with him before he dies. Make it memorable for him. Make his last moments special."

She ran out of my arms into his and gave him tons of kisses. He embraced them all. As each moment went on, I could see the pain in his face and his soul slowly drifting. Madison came to stay with him as we were leaving.

"Okay, I will be back later on today. Please, Christopher, don't die on me until then." We embraced, face-to-face, and he gave me a long slow kiss.

"I think I can wait a few more hours. Thank you, Valerie, I will wait for you," he said and we raced to the airport.

We got home, I packed a bag, got Marisol settled, made some calls, and was back at the airport. As we still had a few days, Marisol stayed in school. She was on standby.

I arrived back that evening as all was good. Madison sat on the couch, watching movies with Christopher, and he was in good spirits. But he was in pain. His face was melting a bit. He did his best to keep his spirit up.

"Well, hello, looks like you guys are having fun. Good to see." I gave them both kisses as I entered into the house.

"Hey, Valerie, thank you for coming back. I really appreciate it. Okay, Dad, I am going home now. Valerie can take you from here. I will be back tomorrow." Madison left and waved from the car. We were back alone and in an awkward silence.

"How are you feeling?"

"I feel okay. I think. I don't know anymore. I am just so happy that you are here with me. So right now, I have all the strength in the world. So Valerie, what are you going to do with me?"

"Look at you, are you hitting on me right now?"

"Yes," he said and pulled me into him on the couch. He kissed me another long slow kiss and pressed me into him.

"You are not well enough for that. Frisky, look at you."

"Valerie, I had you once. Once. We had a beautiful child together. Give me a gift. I always want to remember what it is like to feel you again. Please, Valerie. I have strength today. I may not tomorrow. Valerie, I want you so bad. Humor this old weak man. Give him what he has dreamed about for years."

I looked into his eyes and could see a twinkle in them. "Do what you need to do on Earth, Valerie. I will be waiting for you," I heard Dylan say.

* * * * *

Dylan sat on the floor in his bedroom. He cracked open a beer and held in the upset. He was still understanding. Dylan turned his head and floated into his own memories of us. He floated into the farm. The night I told him I was pregnant with Marisol, he was elated. We danced on the porch and he took such gentle care of me. He kissed my shoulders that stuck out of my sundress, and when we went upstairs, he untied it and it fell to the floor. He took me to the mirror and rubbed my stomach and made me watch. He caressed my body and he told me how much he loved me, us. He went to his knees to give me pleasure in appreciation.

His taste was so warm. He was so grateful. He saw himself in Marisol. He gave himself to us. He made her who she is today, a beautiful sassy girl turning into a beautiful smart woman. He smiled as he was proud to have that.

*   *   *   *   *

I kissed Christopher back and leaned further in to feel his body. "Wow, kid, you really are up for the challenge."

"Valerie, you have no idea."

He pushed me down into the couch, took our clothes off, and did what he dreamed about doing to me for all the years that had passed.

We laid on the adjacent couches and held our fingers as we looked into each other.

"It all starts tomorrow. Valerie, you made me so happy. I am ready to go. You gave me everything I need."

I held his finger and massaged it without responding. I didn't know what to say. I got up and walked over to the back window, looking at the golf course. He came up behind me and kissed my shoulders. We didn't need words. He moved his hands to my waist. He kissed my body as if he wanted to remember each piece.

"Get dressed," I said to him.

"What? Why?"

"Just do it. Let's do this." I smacked his knee and I also got dressed and opened up a bottle of wine and dragged him out the back door into the golf cart; and we went to the eighth hole and played some twilight golf.

"All right, I like this!"

We made fun of each other's swings. We drank wine, and as we came back to his house to the final hole, the sun started to show its face. We sat into each other on the back porch and lit the fire.

"That was great, Valerie. Thank you."

I was at a loss for words. The sun came up. The hospice care set up shop. We sat and we waited. Colby came over. Madison came over. His ex-wife came over. We all sat and stared at each other, waiting for him to just disintegrate.

"All right, people. Let's come on. Let's have some fun. Who wants to play Texas Hold'em? Come on!"

I went to find some cards, got out some liquor, made some snacks, and not before long, we sat at the table and threw around fake coins. We laughed. Christopher laughed. We smoked cigars, made fun of each other. We had an enjoyable day into evening.

That night, I made Christopher's favorite, a steak, but he had trouble eating. He was getting tired. He had trouble standing up. I took him to bed where he hunched over and quickly fell asleep. I played with his hair. I scratched his back, and when he went into a snore, I let him be.

"Madison, we have to find your sister. Can you get her to come?"

"Ugh. I have been trying. She just won't."

"Damn it. She really should be here."

"I will keep trying, I promise."

"Thank you, Madison. I am going to have Marisol come tomorrow. I think this fade is going to be fast."

"Yeah, I see it."

One by one, they left for the evening. His ex-wife asked me to share a glass of wine with her. We didn't have much conversation. This was the first time I ever met her. She was smart and very attractive. I was trying not to be so jealous of her.

"I'm not coming back. This is my goodbye to him."

"What? Why?"

"I am just done. He was such a difficult person. He really made me miserable. I am sad for him, but what he asks of all of us is so much. I am just done with him. You are a loving person to be here. Maybe I am not as much."

"Please reconsider. He did love you. I am sorry you did not have a good experience with him. Please forgive him. In his last moments, please forgive him."

"I can't, Valerie, I just can't. I am going to go and say my goodbye while he is asleep. Because my anger at him has not gone away." She was not asking for permission or going to apologize for it. She went in and said a few words. She kissed his head and waved goodbye as she left. *I am so sad for anyone who has hatred in their heart. It reminds me of Sheila. She will have to learn the hard way.* I prayed for her.

I curled into bed with Christopher as I was still able to. He didn't move much. His body was hard and did not respond to me as I moved about the bed to situate myself around him. I felt him slowly drifting away from us.

"Dylan, please take care of him when he gets there?" I asked. I could still see him sitting on the floor in his bedroom, drinking beer and on a mission to keep his emotions to himself.

"*Mi amor*, whatever you need. I will do it for you. Christopher, hi, it's Dylan. Ask for me when you get here. We have an extra bedroom you can stay in. It's not so bad here. Weather's always good. Food's always available. I drink beer, do you?"

"I can drink beer. But maybe scotch? Thanks, man, this is very kind of you."

"Thank Valerie, she asked me to. She is on loan, you know."

"I know. I am very grateful. Thank you, Dylan. I will see you soon."

The next day was not as easy. Christopher had a hard time getting out of bed and his face sank deeper than the day before. He was struggling. I did my best to coddle him. I rubbed his back as he built the strength to get up out of the bed. "Thanks, Valerie, you are very kind."

"I just want you to be comfortable. What do you need?"

"I don't know. I am ready for some pain meds, I think."

I asked the nurse if she could give him something, which she did.

"Do you want to eat something? What can I get for you?"

"Valerie, no, I don't think I could eat something right now. I just want to lay here and rest.

"You got it."

He sat himself back and drifted into sleep. *I hope that Marisol will be here soon, before he drifts further away.*

After some time, Colby came in. He went into his room and tried to talk to him as he drifted in and out of sleep. Everyone in the house was pacing and taking time to say prayers to themselves. I wanted them to have the proper time alone with him. I went to go in to check on him.

"How are you? What can I get for you?"

"Marisol. Is she coming?"

"Yes, Christopher, she will be here soon. Her plane landed forty minutes ago. She is on her way. What do you need?"

"I need more pain meds. Can you sit with me?" The nurse allowed him for more morphine, and once it sank in, he sat back holding my hands.

"The pain is so strong today," he said. He looked into my eyes that started to become glassy. He was drifting.

Marisol made her way to the house and came into the bedroom.

"Hey princess," he said as he followed her voice. I let her replace my seat and went to go into the other room with Colby. We all did this dance of going from room to room, spending time with him, holding his hand, brushing his hair back, saying goodbye one by one—several times throughout the next day or two. One morning, we sat in his room in a circle telling stories about Christopher, laughing and slapping each other to contain the rambunctious atmosphere.

"I'm so happy, I'm so happy," Christopher said to himself. We could not hear him. He opened his eyes one last time. He saw a blurry vision of us all together, laughing, smiling, celebrating his life. "I'm so happy, I'm so happy," he kept chanting. He closed his eyes and concentrated on the laughter. Soon, the laughter faded away. We were disturbed by the harmonious long beep that silenced the room.

* * * * *

Dylan fell asleep by the window and was awakened by the doorbell ringing. He was startled and saw his new visitor and waved from upstairs. "Okay," he said to himself. He wiped his hand down his face to wake up before he brushed his hand through his hair. His shirt was still the same t-shirt he was wearing for the past few days. He was too upset to change.

He walked in the other bedroom to see Peanut sleeping peacefully and rubbed her check as she smiled in her rest. Dylan ran down the stairs to the door, and with a reluctant smile, he welcomed Christopher into his home and gave him a welcoming brotherly hug.

"Thanks, man, this means a lot."

"Yeah, bro. I get it. You will be happy here, I promise."

"I already am."

As Dylan was the man of this house, he felt it was okay to move himself into the master bedroom and leave the room he occupied for Christopher. They settled their things. Peanut woke up and Dylan brought them both to daily mass.

When they walked home, he showed him the neighborhood. He introduced him to Cal and soon to the rest of the family. Madeline came over that afternoon with a welcoming bunt cake that she was famous for. "Gentlemen, please come over for dinner tonight. I will make some steaks and we can all get to know each other."

"Thank you, Madeline, that is so kind of you," Christopher said.

Madeline nodded and fixed her blouse and touched her curls to make sure they were still intact. She was nervous around Christopher.

"Okay, then. It is settled. I will see you later." She walked backwards then turned to walk as fast as she could across the street.

Christopher stood up from his chair on the lawn, and in astonishment, he called back out to her. "Wait, Madeline. Madeline?"

She turned herself around, holding her hands to her stomach as it was dropping. "Yes?" she said. "Yes." She nodded and went back into her house, ran up the stairs, and when no one could hear her, she sighed in happiness.

Christopher stood on the lawn and tried to figure it out. Then he saw it. He saw her walking down the stairs, coming home from the hospital with Sheila, and remembered shedding many tears and moving far, far away, never seeing them again. He remembered his life before being Christopher. He remembered Madeline.

"You all right, bro?" Dylan said as he came behind him, putting his arm over his shoulder and handing him a drink.

Christopher could not move. He stood there in astonishment. He held his hands to his stomach just as she did and felt her in his body. He could smell her again. He remembered Madeline.

"Bro?"

"Oh, oh, my, I need to sit down." Christopher was starting to get weak and they both moved back into their chairs.

Dylan never took his hand off his shoulder. He gave him time to gather his thoughts and emotions. "A lot happens up here. It's all good, just go with it," Dylan said as he knew his own revelations that had happened.

"I think I just had a miracle happen. This has all been a miracle. Holy shit. How crazy is this? Wow, wow, wow." Christopher grabbed Dylan by the face and gave him a hard kiss and sat back in his chair, suddenly a jittery teenage boy. "Can you help me with something to wear tonight? Help me get some flowers?" Christopher said as he stood up and paced in the short space between the chairs.

"Of course, yes. We can have and get whatever we want up here. Are you okay? I know it is a lot all at once when you get up here. So much to process. Sit, relax, we can do it all. You will get it all. Don't worry, she isn't going anywhere. She remembers you too. It doesn't go away, ever. So don't worry. God is guiding you and will you be okay. Just relax," Dylan said as he got him to sit back down.

Christopher sat back and took some deep breaths and relaxed himself. "It is all going to be okay," he chanted to himself.

*   *   *   *   *

Marisol decided on Duke for college. It really was the best choice for what she wanted. She had a cheerleading scholarship, a scholarship for her good grades. She felt at home on the beautiful North Carolina campus.

I was happy since Duke was Dylan's favorite college basketball team. We went to a few games during March Madness. He insisted that we all attend. He made us paint our faces; that was Pri's favorite part. She made one of her famous signs and we all lived in the glory of watching Dylan scream through the game; and when they won, I had a night I could not forget alone with him.

"Dang, girl, good choice," I said to myself when she told me of her final decision. I remembered each time we came home from that victory. I remembered Dylan's joy and laughter. *Oh, Dylan, I miss you so.*

The house was not lonely this time around without Marisol. The house felt harmonious. I listened to the creaks and appliances sing their songs, and I knew each time it was a message from my loved ones talking to me. I felt fulfilled. Frannie started to help be a stronger part of the farm as I ran the backend and we hired a few new people. We met almost every morning at the kitchen island to have breakfast together and discuss the events of the day. She was a sharp woman, even at her age. She kept those men in check.

I was more comfortable behind the scenes. I moved myself around the farm during the day to spend time at the right moments with all the glory this place offered. Mornings on the island, late morning on the couch, afternoons on the deck late afternoons with Pri in the stall's when she brushed the horses.

"Valerie, come and touch Archie. He is trying to talk to you."

"Hi, Archie," I said and got up from the haystack and went over to press my face next to him. He was so warm and loving. I forget sometimes about the warmth of an animal. He pushed back into me. It made me feel safe. It made me feel whole and peaceful.

Pri was so in tune with the animals. I didn't have as much of a connection. She loved unconditionally. She was my greatest teacher. "Archie is sick, Valerie. Give him some positive energy," she asked of me.

"Oh no, Archie, what is wrong?" I asked.

"I think he has an infection. He is weak today. The doctor is coming this afternoon," Pri said. We rubbed Archie and awaited the doctor to arrive.

I fell asleep in the back of that stall as Dr. Luke came later than expected. I was awakened by him touching my leg. "Sorry to startle you, Valerie. I just wanted to let you know that I was here." It was early evening, and Dr. Luke was stuck all day with a sick cow on the other side of town. He checked Archie's vitals and was able to give him some medication to clear out the infection.

"She is good," he said.

"Who is?" I asked.

"Pri. She is very aware of all the animals on this farm. Her intuition is amazing. This could have dragged out for months before someone found this, and it would have been too late. She just saved his life."

I wanted to cry. *I love Pri, she is so warm-hearted. She is such an amazing human being that I wish I could be. She just saved Archie. That girl has a gift.*

"I like to think that she has a gift from God," I told Dr. Luke.

"I like to think that too," he said to me.

He has such a dashing smile. His steel gray hair, his beard perfectly groomed. His sleeves rolled up just at the right spot below his elbow. His arms were strong. You could see the muscles take hold of his shirt. For the first time, I noticed Dr. Luke.

"Hey, Dr. Luke. It's late and I know you live about forty minutes away. Why don't you stay and have dinner?" I asked and didn't even know where I was going with this.

"That would be lovely, Valerie. Thank you."

I think we both blushed, and I excused myself to run to the house and gather something together for a proper meal. I was blushing. I was nervous. I think I liked Dr. Luke. He came in, and as he is no stranger to our home, the door slammed and I was startled out of excitement.

"Hello, Valerie?" He walked around the downstairs looking for me. He found the pasta boiling on the stove, the chicken cutlets in the frying pan. He caught me as I was upstairs adjusting my bra, putting on lipstick, and spraying new perfume.

"Hi, Dr. Luke! I will be down in one sec. Can you open some wine please?"

"Yes, of course, take your time, Val." He went to open a bottle of wine, and as the cork popped open, I looked into the mirror and spoke to Dylan.

"Dyl, are you okay with this? You said have a life. Is this okay?"

Dylan sat on the lawn with Christopher and they drank their beverages, and he was listening to Christopher ramble about how beautiful Madeline was.

"*Si, si.* I like Luke, he is a good guy. Please, yes. Go and have a life. I will be here. Remember, you are out on a loan."

"I love you, Dylan, that will never change."

"Valerie, I know. You don't have to remind me each time. I know. You are in my heart."

I blew a kiss and went downstairs to enjoy dinner and conversation with a gorgeous man.

"Valerie, I flipped the chicken and drained the pasta. I hope that is okay?"

"Oh, yes, thank you, Dr. Luke. You are so sweet. Sorry, I am a bit flaky today.

"No, you are not. And please, you don't have to call me Dr. Luke."

"Right. Right. I am sorry. I—"

He grabbed my hand, and with the other, he gave me a glass of wine.

"Drink, don't apologize. You are all good."

We cheered glasses, ate dinner at the island by candlelight, and drank more wine. We talked business. He told me about why he became a vet. I just listened. I gazed into his eyes. He gazed into mine. His chair came closer to mine on the island. I poured more wine. His hands found their way to my knee. I found my way to touch his forearm that was so masculine and defined by muscles. His body was warm. His smile was kind. I never looked at him this way before. He ate breakfast at my house with Dylan so many mornings. He came over for dinner so many evenings. We had Christmas together for years and years. I never looked at him this way. His hair was thick and such a perfect length that, after a few glasses of wine, I had the nerve to run my fingers through it. He smiled, and as I came to the back of his head, his hand reached for my wrist and he kissed it. I blushed.

"Valerie, I have had such a crush on you for years."

"What? Seriously? I really had no idea."

"Why do you think my wife left me? No, no. I am kidding. I left her. She cheated on me."

"Dr. Luke… I mean, Luke, I am so sorry. I never asked. I had no idea."

"It is fine. I didn't come here to talk about her. She is the past. I am so happy for the future. But I will tell you, I told Dylan all the time I was so jealous of him for having you. I was so jealous of what you had."

I blushed and was taken aback by his words. I let him kiss my wrist again. The piece that was open between my palm and where Dylan's watch was stuck. I drifted into that tingle it gave me. He looked into my eyes and I smiled.

"Dylan always liked you. Pri likes you so much. And…"

"Valerie, stop talking. I know they do. I like them too. Valerie, do you like me?"

I smirked and giggled a bit. "Why, Dr. Luke… Luke… I do think I like you." I placed my finger on his lips and I could taste his heat.

"Good because, Valerie, if it is not obvious at this time, this moment… I like you too. I wanted this moment for a long time.

Thank you, Dylan, I will not know how to repay you." As he opened his mouth to say these words, I could feel the wet on his lips, the vibration from his vocals. I moved in to taste it, and Luke gave me a kiss.

It was short. It was slow. It was hard. It was so tasty. We stopped and pressed our heads together to take a moment and embrace the intensity. It was intense.

"Valerie," he said with his eyes closed. Mine were closed too.

"*Si?*"

"Are you okay with this? Are you ready for this? Do you want this?"

"*Si.*"

"Are you sure?"

"Luke, enough. Stop talking and take me upstairs." He was gentle. He took his time. He was so loving and not able to hit every avenue the first trial. So he went again and again. He took such care of me. For the next few hours, I didn't think about Dylan. I relaxed. I had feeling. I smiled again. I was not alone.

The next morning, I awoke to a new man in my bed where Dylan used to sleep. As awkward as it sounds saying it out loud, it wasn't. Dylan was fine with it. He had a new bed now where he waited for me. I awoke to a gorgeous man smiling into his pillow, smiling back at me, touching my face, touching my body. We didn't need words.

"What will Pri think?" he said with a giggle and pulled me to him and gave me a kiss. I pushed myself up on him and sat on his chest and basked in his beauty.

"Hmmm… she is very intuitive. I am sure she will tell us what this is about before we figure it out."

"That sounds like the Pri I know."

We laughed and kissed and touched for a few more minutes. Then the door slammed. It was Frannie waiting on her morning briefing.

"Valerie? Valerie?" she called out and we giggled.

"And now we are caught," I whispered in his ear as she felt no need to be polite and ask for permission to come into my room.

"Valerie?" she said with anger, expecting me to be in bed alone with probably a bottle of tequila and expecting me to be in misery, and she would have to pick up the slack on the farm and nurse me at the same time.

"Valerie! Dr. Luke! Oh, my, oh. Wow. Okay! I am so sorry."

We laughed as she was embarrassed. "Frannie, can you give us a few minutes?"

"OMG! Yes. Yes. Oh, my gosh." She put her hand on her eyes and paced in and out of the door in embarrassment.

"Frannie?"

"*Si, si.* OMG!" She ran back down the stairs and into her house and held Pri back from coming into the home. Luke and I laughed so hard and he pulled me back in for another replay of the night before. We laughed and laughed. It was such the stress relief. It was just what we both needed and wanted. It was perfect.

*　　*　　*　　*　　*

Christopher was so nervous. He wanted to count the minutes that did not exist in heaven. He could not wait to see Madeline again. His nervousness was a thing of the past he was working on letting go of.

"Christopher, I have the roses for you. Did you want red? Come into my room. I have a nice shirt and we can make sure you look your best. Look at us, a couple of chicks trying to get a man. Ha-ha."

Christopher laughed at Dylan's joke and felt better about the situation. They went upstairs into Dylan's room that at one point in time was once Christopher's, and on some occasions, Christopher and Madeline's.

"Valerie one time called herself a man during a fight and made me laugh. It was so funny. She was the best," Dylan said as he sized up Christopher to the proper shirt.

"She was the best. When are we going to talk about her?" Christopher asked as he wanted the elephant to leave the room.

"No need. No need. Whatever you want to know, just ask me. I understand there are questions. I have some too. We will get there. Just know, I am grateful. I forgive. Valerie is in my heart. No one will change that." Dylan was not changing his mind. I wasn't either.

* * * * *

Luke and I showered together, which was really just giggling and using soap as an excuse to touch each other. He pushed me away from the sink as we brushed our teeth, and all I could do was laugh. Oh, it feels so good to laugh again. I made breakfast and let Frannie know it was okay to come back. I was cooking eggs. He was sipping coffee as he stood close enough to the stove with his back at the counter to watch me. The door slammed; it was Frannie.

"Hi, y'all," she said with embarrassment and a blush.

"Hello." We replied but didn't take attention to that direction. She took a seat at the island and as soon as I was serving, Pri came and ran to sit next to her.

"Dr. Luke! You came back to check on Archie?" Pri asked in excitement that someone cared with such detail about the animals as she did. He sat and sipped his coffee. Frannie and I tried to catch his eye before he responded.

As he opened his mouth, he caught the hint and just replied, "Oh, yes, Pri, I of course want to make sure he is responding to his meds."

I mouthed a thank you to him and he smiled back. Breakfast was done, and Pri begged Dr. Luke to walk with her to the stable and visit Archie. As she grabbed his hand, he spilled the last sip of his coffee on his recycled shirt and ran with her. The door slammed again. Then Frannie moved her attention to invade my personal space.

"Valerie, you dirty girl. Good for you! So tell me everything!" She was genuinely happy for this to happen. I didn't know how to stop from being so elated with happiness.

"I don't know, Frannie. I was in the stable and fell asleep working, and he woke me up and dang, girl, he is so freaking sexy standing over me. I was like a school girl. I am a giggling teenager. I don't know how to stop being so freakin' happy!"

"I love this! How wonderful for you to find each other. He is a kind, kind soul."

"He is, isn't he?"

"Yes, his wife was horrible to him what she did. He was really hurt."

"So what happened? I mean, I knew they got divorced years ago, but I don't know why. I just never asked. Dylan was close with him, not me. Of course, Dylan wouldn't gossip or pry into his life so I didn't know."

"I don't know all the details. It is his story to tell, if and when he wants to. But it is in the past. From the look on both of your faces, it looks like a mutual connection. I like it. Now to your bigger problem."

"What problem? Why, what happened?"

"Pri."

"What happened? Is this another 'I am a horrible mother' moment? What did I miss?"

"Valerie, don't you remember? Pri has a huge crush on Dr. Luke! I mean, who doesn't? But she doesn't understand. Remember?"

"Oh, yeah. Oh, gosh, I forgot. She doesn't understand. He is so good to her. I hate secrets, I really do. I mean, I don't know, was this just a one night thing? Why do we have to tell her? I mean, ugh. I don't know. I don't know."

"Girl, look at your glow. Go and look in the mirror right now and look at your glow. I think it is more than a one night thing. And you do deserve it, so don't let this stop you. Let's just think of how we can let her find out gently. She lives with me, so for now you can sneak around until you do."

"Thank you, Frannie. I really needed that. I am so lucky to have you. I am glad that I have your blessing on this. He is so damn sexy. I can't take it. I never looked at him like this before. I just want to grab him and jump him. Man."

"You are a frisky teenager. Good for you," she said and smacked my ass. *Why does she keep doing that?*

"Frannie? Why did you never marry again? Why didn't you find someone else?"

"There was someone else. There was, there is. I am not as sweet and innocent as I look."

"Frannie! Who? When and where do you... Frannie!" I was pushing her shoulder as she had some milk to spill.

"Now, now, girl, I am not telling you all my business!"

As we continued our probing and taunting, the door slammed again. We were wrestling and poking each other and eventually just hugging in excitement for each other. And now wrestling in the living room. We were teenagers again.

"What is wrong with you ladies?" As Luke stood over us with his sharp glasses, wood-edged, arms crossed, sleeves rolled up, and showed his sharp muscles on shine, he pretended to scold us. But all we could do was laugh harder. He was so sexy. He laughed back and helped us get up. We still couldn't stop and kept pushing each other as we stumbled back to the island.

"You ladies are hysterical right now. Did you start drinking already?"

We ignored him. It only made us laugh harder.

He went back to his coffee and watched us. "Crazy kids."

*   *   *   *   *

"So what time are we going over there? Is it now?" Christopher was so nervous.

"Bro, relax. Relax! It's all good."

"Dylan, I was so in love with her. I had to leave. The pain was too much to watch. I don't remember anything else but pain. Dylan, what do I do?"

Dylan listened tentatively and held Christopher's shoulder. He smiled as he understood what it meant. "Love. Isn't that what you want? To love her and to be loved?"

"Yes, but..."

"Yes, but what?"

"She is married. She has a family. Now what?" Christopher remembered being with his wife when they were married. After they had Madison, they shared a big house together in Reston, Virginia. It was so big they could hide from each other and not even hear the other scream. It was a palace. They made it into their prison. They didn't have dinner together. Christopher worked late and came home drunk. She stayed home with the girls and gave up her job before Christopher made her happy.

He made nasty comments to her about the Amex bill and how she ate to many cookies, telling her how it showed as he touched her sides and pinched a part of her skin as hard as he could. He demanded that she was his escort at corporate events and put her down in front of his colleagues. She giggled to brush it off, but it hurt. It really hurt. When they came home, Christopher headed to his study and poured another scotch for himself. He sat alone and cursed her out as she could hide in so many crevasses in that house. She stood outside the door and listened. She shed silent tears. When his vision was blurry, when he forgot his own name, he stumbled into the bed that she just entered into and pretended she had been there the whole time.

The sheets were cold. She curled herself into the far corner. He took off his clothes and fell into the bed, making it jump a bit. He pulled the sheets to him. She tried to hold onto a piece to keep from being cold. He still managed to tear that piece away from her. She shed more silent tears but did not move or fight to get the sheets back. She laid there cold. He started to snore away after a few moments, and in the morning with his awful breath, he pulled himself over onto her and slid himself into her, dry and painful. He did not ask for permission nor apologize for it. After years of this, she just gave in, held her breath from smelling his, tightened her eyes from watching the act, and prayed for it to just go away as quickly as possible.

She was a powerful lawyer that held the attention of every man in a courtroom. In her own bedroom, she had no power. No conversation nor affection with the man she married. There were no words exchanged. No kisses exchanged. No "thanks yous" exchanged. Christopher jumped into the shower. She put her clothes on to make breakfast and started the cycle over again.

"I was a horrible person," Christopher said to himself in the mirror. "Please forgive me." He called out to her. She looked up as she drove to work that morning, looked through the sunroof, and shook her head no. The reminder of those moments gave her a shock; each time, she had to shake her body to get the tingle out.

"No," she said.

"I don't blame you," he said back. He would try this cycle again soon.

He went back to Dylan and tried to push away the memory as he entered into a past one that became new. He remembered the last days of his life—Valerie singing in his ear and brushing his hair back as he drifted away from his life on Earth. She was his angel that led him back to Madeline.

"Christopher, you are in heaven now. The game has changed. This is the place where it all gets worked out. There is no hatred up here. Only love. So love her. There is no judgment here. There is only joy. Just let God lead the way. He will. Love and accept love. Everything is provided for. You are here for a reason."

Christopher took a deep breath and sat down again. He looked at himself in the mirror and saw the young man he was from the life he had when he met Madeline. He wasn't the Christopher he just left. He was grateful as that person was fading from that image. That person hurt people, made him feel lonely, made the people around him feel alone. He felt alive again.

"Dylan, you are the best. So kind. Valerie is so lucky to have met you."

"You are right. She is lucky she met me." And they both laughed.

The giggles continued and relaxed. It didn't change the smiles on their face.

*   *   *   *   *

"Frannie has been cheating on me," I said to Luke as he was so delightfully confused as to what was going on. We continued to giggle. He sipped his coffee and gave his, "Um-huh."

"Okay, ladies, okay. You are seriously cracking me up here. Seriously. Ladies, Valerie, we have a problem." He drew me into him as he placed me onto his lap so we could separate, and he then had an excuse to touch me and stop me from slapping Frannie.

"Yeah, so she gave me a card today telling me how she feels about me and wants to be my girlfriend. Now I love her, you both know that I do. She does try to tell me as often as possible how much she likes me. I am polite, it is super innocent what she is thinking. But now, I can't take my hands off of this wonderful woman. I don't want to hurt her feelings. Can we work on a plan here?"

"What plan? Do you have plans with someone else that she should worry about?" Frannie said in sarcasm. I reached to smack her as Luke held me back.

"Yes, I do. I like this lady in my arms right now. I plan on holding her down as long as I am strong enough to hold her. So yes, Frannie. I want to be with this Valerie in my arms for a very long time." We all smiled and I moved in to kiss his cheek, and Frannie came over to kiss his other cheek.

"So what are we going to do?" he asked and welcomed all the kisses from us crazy ladies.

"Valerie?" Frannie looked at me. "I know, I know. It is my problem. I am so bad when it comes to her. I am so sensitive to hurting her feelings. I am such a disappointment to handling her. But yes, I took on the job to be her mother, so I need to make a choice. Okay. Okay. I will talk to her and feel it out. Can we ease her into it? Wait! What exactly am I easing her into. Luke?"

"Valerie, I am never letting go of you. Do you want me to let go of you?"

"No."

"All right. So yes, we need to figure that out. So if we are not letting of each other anytime soon, we need to tell Pri and not do a Zavala 'Oh shit, you figured that out?' game."

Dang, he knows me better than I know myself. Oh Luke, you are so sexy when you are wise.

"Valerie, stop it. She has a life and would be far worse in Mexico. This isn't a time for it to be a blame issue. I will not tiptoe around this so… are you going to talk to her and say what?"

"She usually tells me in verbatim about her day. So if she doesn't mention it, maybe I'll ask her about Archie then segue into you, Luke? Tell her that I like Luke very much and start from what her reaction will be? I think she doesn't know how to take it further than that. Oh, I love her so much. I so don't want to hurt her feelings."

"I think that is a good place," Frannie said.

Luke held me close and nibbled on my neck which made me lose concentration and giggle uncontrollably.

"Hmmm. Well, all right. But dang it, I will have to be here a lot to take care of that Archie. And maybe you might get sick too, Valerie? I just want to be a full service to the Zavala family."

He was so delicious. I couldn't get enough of him. We all had to go on with our day and I said goodbye to Luke in the kitchen, who agreed to come back that night for dinner. Oh, his kisses were long and intense. His hold was just enough. His memory carried me through the day. I had a job in front of me. *Now how to best tackle it?* I needed to think.

* * * * *

They walked over to Cal and Madeline's where Christopher was sweating and Dylan was laughing and holding Peanut. He kept his hand on Christopher's back, reassuring him that it would be okay. He was still laughing. Cal met them at the door, open arms and hugs. They entered into the kitchen through to the back where all the ladies held court. Christopher ran in his awkward boy run toward Madeline, who was also nervous, and handed her the flowers he requested for her.

"Flowers are so much more lovely in heaven than they are on Earth. Thank you, Christopher," Madeline said and smelled them to enjoy the extra beauty they gave. He enjoyed watching her take in the fumes.

"All right, boys, beer? Wine? Christopher, I believe you said Scotch was your drink?"

"Oh, yes sir, thank you so much. Scotch is lovely." They sat down at the back porch and enjoyed the fire. Madeline flipped the steaks.

"So nice of you all to go through so much trouble for us today," Christopher said in his nervous state. Cal poured drinks and handed them out. No one said a word.

"Christopher. No need to be so nervous. We all know. We all accept. We all understand. It is all okay. God is good. Let him lead you to it being okay," Cal said to him.

Dylan put his arm over Cal, cheered drinks, and nodded. "See, I told you. We all understand. We all know everything. It is a gift. Be okay with what happened. Forgive. It will all be okay," Dylan added.

Madeline served dinner and sat next to Christopher close enough that her knee touched his. He was still so nervous.

"I missed you," she whispered in his ear. Everyone else moved their conversation to something else. He stopped chewing and looked around. They did not give him attention. He focused on her.

"I wanted you to choose me. I wanted you to stay with me. Have a child with me. You made a choice. I couldn't live with it. I couldn't watch. You and Cal had a beautiful girl together. I was so jealous of it. I just couldn't watch."

"Cal and I didn't have a child together."

"What? Yes, you did."

"Christopher. Christopher. Did you meet Sheila?"

"Yes, I did. She is right there. She is just as beautiful as you are." The crowd turned to them as they spoke. He didn't know.

*   *   *   *   *

I went to bring Pri a sandwich as she was perched with Archie and so concerned about how he was progressing. *She's a bit obsessed with this one. He is going to be just fine.*

"Hey, Pri, how are you doing in here?"

"Archie is going to be okay."

"That is great, Pri. I am sure that Dr. Luke knows what he is doing for sure."

"Yup, Valerie. I asked Dr. Luke on a date."

"You did? What did he say?"

"He said that he was going to think about it. I really like him, Valerie."

"Oh, that is sweet, Hun. I really like him too. I like him so much. So when you take him on a date, what are you going to do?"

"I will make him a tea party and then a walk on the farm."

"That sounds like a lovely date. So what else do you want from Dr. Luke?"

"A hug."

"Just a hug? That is so nice, Pri. I think that is lovely. I like Dr. Luke too. I think that he and I are going to go on a date too. Will you be okay with that? I didn't know you had already asked him. I want to have nice dinners with him and go dancing sometimes. Spend lots and lots of time with him. Have sleepovers with him. So we can both have what we want. How do you feel about that?"

"I think that is okay. Will you take care of him when he gets sick? Like make him chicken soup like you did for Dylan? How you made him stay in bed and feed him?"

"Oh, I forgot about that! Oh, yes, Pri. I will take care of him when he gets sick and all the other fun things that go with that."

"Okay, I love you, Valerie!"

"Oh, Pri, I love you too." I gave her a hug and went back to the house. Frannie stood in the kitchen.

"So? How did it go?"

"Well, I think it went okay. She just wants to have a tea party with him and a hug. I told her that I wanted to be with him also. Have dinners, blah, blah, blah. Said we can both have that. She ran with it. I think we are in the clear."

"Wow, smart move. Yeah, that should work!" She came over and gave me a hug. "Oh, Valerie. I am so happy for you."

"Oh, Frannie, maybe one day we can meet your boyfriend?"

"Oh, Valerie. Maybe it's not a boy."

"*Ooohhhhhh...*" I said. Well, I never thought of other options.

That night, Luke came over for dinner with a bag packed to stay for a few days.

"Well, you know, I have to look over Archie and all. I want to be close by," he said as he dropped his bag and came in for a kiss. He was so delicious. We laughed, we kissed. His arms were so strong. I was enjoying being in them. "I was afraid of where this Pri direction was. But I can live with these terms."

Oh, Luke, you are my favorite distraction.

Frannie took me in town to do a stupid painting party night—drink wine and paint something. *Whatever.* She insisted. I was not so into it, but as Frannie and I grew closer, I wanted to be supportive. I noticed her and the instructor having a bond. Then I felt the tension. *Oh, now I get why we are here.* She was very attractive. Older, like Frannie. She had silky white hair that she kept super straight. She let it dangle on Frannie's shoulders as she leaned in to help her with her strokes. Frannie moved her head to have it touch her shoulder. They did not look at each other. I stopped to take notice, watch Frannie stop, and watch Albina as she walked about the room helping others. Frannie had on a smile that was in a deep thought somewhere else. Somewhere with Albina.

After class, Frannie introduced me to Albina and they giggled at each other. Frannie hung on every word she said. I never saw this side of her. She for sure had a crush, perhaps something even more than that. They said goodbye with a long tight hug and a linger of letting go of each other's arms. It ended with an air kiss. Frannie and I went home in silence as she was still in her daydream. When we got to the farm, Frannie invited me for a walk.

We walked arm in arm, in big sweaters as the night air had a chill to it.

"Some nights, Dylan and I came out for a walk," Frannie said to me.

"Really? I don't think I knew that. Wow, that is so nice. I am glad."

"Oh, Dylan, he was a warm heart. Valerie, he so loved you."

"I know, I know. He was the best. I wish I was better to him."

"Now, stop it. That is nonsense. None of us are perfect."

"I know, I know. So what did you and Dylan talk about?"

"Oh, life, the farm, you, the kids… he got mad at himself. He missed Olivia so much and cried. When he was mad at you for doing something or when he thought he failed you, it was just Dylan being sensitive and needing his momma." She shed a tear that she whipped away before I could see it.

"He came to me in a dream the other day, Valerie. He asked me to watch over you and let you know it is okay to be with Luke."

"He told me the same thing."

"Good. Good. That Luke, woohoo. Sexy doctor. Don't they have a TV show about that?"

"I think there are several TV shows about hot doctors. Oh, he is a sexy one for sure. I am really lucky. I am so blessed. My life has been a wild rollercoaster ride. Now I feel good and content. I am happy where I am in my life right now."

"That is great, Valerie. Good. I am content too."

"Yes, I can see your happiness. Your glow."

"Well, now you know my secret."

"So when? How long? Why haven't I heard about this before?"

"Well, I don't know. I never thought or intended to have a thing for a woman. But I had a husband that was a good man. He took us out of Mexico and brought us here. He built us a dream. He didn't make smart choices for how he went about it. You know the prices we paid. Matteo was at the wrong place at the wrong time. He fought with his heart. We didn't really have a love story. We had a survival story. We had children to have children. We worked hard to feed them. We had a relationship, but it was hard. Not so warm. But I did love him dearly. He is the father of my children and I do love him for that. I love him for the dream he had, and he went after it for us. But we didn't have passion. I always wanted passion.

"I tried to meet another man. I had a few affairs with some of the guys that worked here on the farm. But it was meaningless, and they always saw me as the boss. It felt cheap. There was lust but no passion. I wanted passion.

"I watched you and Dylan. You guys had passion. I saw you from the bedroom window some nights, twirling around the room, and I could hear your laughter, your groans, your passion. For the record, you guys were loud, y'all."

"Frannie! I had no idea! I am so embarrassed!" I tugged away from her a bit as I felt exposed. She pulled me back to her.

"No, no. Don't be. I had no business looking into your windows. I was jealous of what you both had together and just wanted to watch and see if I could feel something again. Learn how to do what you were doing. I was so jealous. In the mornings, when I came over for breakfast, Dylan just watched you with a smirk. When you caught eyes, you both smiled. You have that again with Luke. It is a wonderful thing. Embrace it."

"Ah, Frannie, that is stalker-ish and lovely at the same time. Luke is so much like Dylan, but different. It is really nice to have him. I am so blessed. So tell me more. Tell me about Albina."

"Oh, Valerie. I don't know how it happened, and like I said, I was seeking passion. I wanted to be in a relationship. I wanted to be wanted. I wanted it to be easy. It just hasn't been easy. She sat at my table one morning at the coffee shop in town. I went there from time to time to escape the farm. I was staring out the window, watching the fog lift. She came and sat down in front of me. I didn't see her coming. I turned to her and she smiled. She has a warm smile. She asked me if I was in her yoga class, which I was, and we starting talking. She touched my hand and asked me to come over for dinner that evening. I did. It was just us, set by candle light in her studio. We drank wine, she touched my hand, and after time, she kissed me. My reaction was to hold back, but I didn't. She drew me closer. She took care of me. She touched my breast with such attention and stroked her fingers down them and drew me close. She did things to me I never experienced. I had feelings and emotions I never had before. I felt passion."

"Wow, Frannie. That is so nice. I am really happy for you."

"I am happy for you. I don't talk about her. This is the first time. We are friends, we are passionate friends. I like the distance we have, so when I see her, it is special and not a burden. I like the secret. I like the passion."

"Passion is a good thing. Thank you, Frannie, for telling me your story. I love it." We hugged and went back into our homes.

Dr. Luke sat at the island with his laptop and coffee. "How was your evening with Frannie?" he asked with a smile, and his nerdy glasses made me tingle.

"It was nice. She told me about her lover. She told me that I am very loud when I have sex."

"You are."

"Great, well now I have a complex," I said and turned around to make myself an evening tea. Luke came up behind me and startled me as he held my thighs and nibbled on my neck.

"I didn't say there was anything wrong with it. I think it is sexy, Valerie." The tea could wait as we could not take our hands off of each other. Oh, how those nerdy glasses knew how to dazzle me.

*   *   *   *   *

"I don't know. What am I supposed to know?" Christopher asked, afraid of why everyone was looking at him. Sheila came over to him and held his hand and sat before him. Dylan took Peanut to move out of their way. Ashley, Dylan, and Cal all moved into the living room to give them time alone. Madeline stood behind Sheila. Sheila held his hands tighter and looked into his eyes. She didn't have to say anything.

"OMG, OMG. You are my daughter! I can't believe this. Now I understand. My daughter would not come and see me before I died. She was mad at me, because I left you. She felt it and I didn't even know." Christopher became emotional. He looked down in disappointment.

"Christopher, I didn't know who the father was. I was so nervous of what to do. I wanted it to be you. It was always you. When she was born, I looked into her eyes and I saw you. Then you left. I had no idea how to find you. I was planning to leave Cal and tell him everything to be with you. But you left. I mourned you ever since. I kept lies and anger. We have all forgiven each other now. When you are here, you learn to forgive. Now we can have the relationship we wanted. Christopher, Cal is leaving. He is making his next step. I want to have the relationship with you I always wanted, what you always wanted... what Sheila always wanted."

"This place really is heaven. Wow, wow. Now I know why I met Valerie."

"You met Valerie to find me. You have been found. I love you, Christopher," she said as she touched his face.

"I love you too, Madeline."

Madeline came in and gave him a kiss. He was overjoyed with passion. That night, Madeline went across the street and they went into the third bedroom and closed the door.

*　　*　　*　　*　　*

I blinked my eyes a few times before I woke up this morning. Luke was still asleep and I touched his cheek. He smiled and kissed my palm before he opened his eyes. No glasses, just his hazel eyes glancing back at me. My palm on his scruff was scratchy. I let him suck on my finger before I went in for a kiss. He pulled me onto him and I just laid on his chest and outlined his broad shoulders with my wet index finger. I was so lucky to be here.

I invited Albina to come to dinner with Frannie to enjoy a night with myself and Luke. She made a lemon tart and brought a dry white wine from California. She wore white. She told us it would keep the pureness in her soul open. She was warm and very calm. Us Zavala's seemed to be a lot more intense. When Frannie was around her, she became calm and kind. *Not the bitch I know. Ha!*

"Albina, where are you from?" Luke asked as he opened the bottle of wine.

"I am from California, around the coastline," she answered as she gathered glasses for everyone.

Luke poured the wine. I stood at the stove working on a medium-well salmon. "Hey, no way! I'm from California too! My dad lives in Malibu. We just tell everyone LA."

"That is great! Nice, see, I knew I liked you." She placed her hand on my back as I presented the tray of salmon to the table. We didn't sit much at the table that sat in the big bay window past the kitchen island. I felt so formal having an adult dinner with Frannie and her lover, Luke by my side. No distractions, no insanity—Just us enjoying ourselves.

When dinner was over, we all sat back into each other's partners and drifted in to our own private worlds, daydreaming and whispering about what we wanted to do to our partners after everyone said goodnight. Luke pulled me in for a kiss. Albina pulled Frannie in for a kiss. We retreated to the couches with our coffees and laughed about stories from the farm. It was a wonderful evening. Frannie and I became new friends. Secrets she kept became truths. It was a good day.

My phone and Frannie's phone both dinged at the same time. The door slammed and Pri came running in gasping for breath. Something was wrong.

"Pri, are you okay? Pri? What is going on?"

She had too much to say. She was having an anxiety attack. We all rushed over to her as she held her chest gasping and gasping. Luke took her to check her pulse and calm her. She eventually did. I was so scared and held her arm, my other on his back.

"It's time, it's time! We have to go now!"

We sat there in silence as we didn't know what that meant. Then we remembered.

"OMG! It's time! Clarissa is having the baby!" We ran to our phones and saw the message.

Text from John: "At the hospital now, Clarissa is in labor!"

"John! We are on our way!"

We grabbed the keys and Luke took us all to the hospital. We were able to be there for John and Clarissa. We got there and waited patiently for the news of another Zavala to enter into our world.

$$* \quad * \quad * \quad * \quad *$$

Dylan held Peanut in his arms as he left the house to go to daily mass. Cal came out at the same time and walked with him.

"It is going to be soon. I can feel it," Cal said to Dylan.

"Are you ready?" Dylan asked. He would miss Cal when he moved on.

"I think so. I am ready, it is time to go back. I had what I needed up here and feel good that Christopher and Madeline have found each other again. I have been working with the big man and he let me know I will know when I am ready. I will hear the voices. I haven't yet, but I feel them coming. I believe it is coming."

"Good for you. I am so grateful to have this time with you. Cal, you have helped me so much."

"Thank you, Dylan, I have enjoyed the time spent with you also. Thank you for what you did for Valerie. She really loves you. She was looking for you the whole time. If she didn't search for Christopher, if she didn't go through what she went through, she wouldn't have found her way to you. God is good."

"He is for sure good. I am so grateful to have met Valerie. She is always in my heart. I am watching over her. I want her to be happy. I really want her to be happy in the last stretch of her life. I want to give that to her."

Cal gave Dylan a kiss on his forehead and they went to mass.

*   *   *   *   *

We paced in the waiting room, and somehow Frannie got her hands on a deck of cards. We played gin rummy to anxiously take our minds off of waiting for the baby.

"Do you have kids, Albina?" Luke asked.

I looked intently at her.

"No, no. I decided that I didn't want to have children. Or the decision was made for me. I can't have children."

Frannie rubbed her back and pulled her in for a hug. "Pregnancy was the worst. You didn't miss anything," Frannie said to comfort her.

"I felt like it was so fast for me. I didn't have time to think about it. It was so fast."

I looked at Luke as if he knew the answer to my question.

"I remember you pregnant. You were beautiful," Luke said to me and we smiled and kissed.

"You remember me pregnant?" I said to him.

"Oh, yes. You held it well. You also held it in your ass," he said as he gave it a light smack, and we walked around to the other side of the waiting room to walk around and pass the time. We held hands and wanted to get home to try to make one of our own, even though it was past that time for us.

"So why didn't you have any kids, Luke?"

"Oh, Valerie. That's a loaded question. I just didn't have a great childhood. I didn't want to bring a child into this world and be exposed to that. I just didn't." He was looking down and stopped to look out the window and let go of me as he crossed his arms. I hit a nerve.

"I am sorry, Luke, I didn't know. Do you want to talk about it?" I went up to hug his closed body language and perched on his shoulder. There was a pause. I kept my hold on his and gave him kisses on his cheek and ran my fingers up and down his back. He was really hurt. I could tell. Pri interrupted us as she was bored with the waiting.

"What is up, Pri?" he said and snapped back to himself.

"Valerie, I am bored and tired," she said and came to leg to rest against me.

"Let's go back to the waiting room and rest on the couch."

We walked back. Luke and I held hands and I leaned into him and looked at him and he released a smile. "I'll take care of you," I said to him, and he gave me a kiss.

I feel asleep with Pri resting on my lap and my head resting on Luke's shoulder. He also gazed off. Frannie and Albina sat on the other couch and watched us and smiled.

"You have a loving family, Frannie," Albina said to her.

"I am a lucky lady," Frannie said back.

The door flew open and John came out with a smile. "It's a girl! We have a girl!"

We all jumped up and screamed and hugged. They let us see her through the glass and the next day in the room. Both Clarissa and the baby were just fine. They named the baby Mary as they could not think of any other name that could bring them such joy. She was beautiful.

John and Clarissa lived in town and had us over for family dinners every few weeks. Mary was a few years old, and I still could not believe that I was a grandmother. Luke used it to hit on me when he walked out of the shower and I was still debating about waking up for the day.

"Hey, Grandma, when you going to get out of bed?"

I threw a pillow at him. Each morning before he left for the day, we had a kissing session as if we couldn't get enough of the last kiss. I dreamt all day in the way his kiss felt. He was so delicious and still as sexy as the day I awoke and saw him in this light. The long goodbyes kept me tingled all day. Frannie sat at the island, ready to finish our meeting and sip her coffee.

"You still got it, girl. He is wrapped around your finger," Frannie said.

"I think I may be wrapped around his?" I said and twisted up my hair. I was still in the recent memory of being attached to his lips. "Frannie, I want to throw Luke a surprise birthday party. What do you think?"

"Surprise party! Oh, wow, haven't done one of those in a long time. Remember when you threw Dylan one and he came in when he wasn't supposed to and no one turned around?"

"Oh, my gosh, yes! How old was he? Was it his fortieth? Oh, yes, he was walking around and no one was fazed by it. That was so funny!"

We laughed and drank coffee, started to talk about the farm, and went back to that party. We had such a great night. I had bought enough balloons to fill the entire downstairs. Dylan was finally acknowledged as he found his way to me and came behind me in his sweaty work clothes—his favorite blue and red flannel and his favorite hat. He came behind me and touched my elbows, and I still didn't acknowledge him. He finally pushed himself into my hair and the conversation I was having. I realized he was there. I turned around and screamed out loud, "*Dylan!*" Then the party all looked around and started laughing. Oh, it was such a great party. He was so surprised and had a blast.

I excused myself and went upstairs into the closet and took out his flannel and put it on. I still had Dylan in my heart, but at that moment, I just wanted to feel him again. I put it on and felt his power.

"I miss you too, Valerie, I really do. Don't be sad. Have a life. Give Luke what he needs. Give him a party. You are in my heart, don't lose trust on that. Go and do what you need to do," Dylan said, and it felt good to wear his shirt and remember the party. I went back downstairs and we continued the conversation and laughs. Frannie touched my arm and smiled; she missed him too.

Luke had moved into the house with me a few years ago. It was nice to have someone to share the space with. I enjoyed watching him pull up to the farm as I cooked dinner for us. We caught eyes when he came up to the house and saw me at the stove, and I glanced back at him through the window. The door slammed as he entered the room. He was so infectious. We never stopped having the passion Frannie wished on.

That Saturday, I had planned for Luke's surprise birthday party. I was so excited to do this for him. We invited all of his patients as he had not much of a family, but he had ours. I wanted it to be perfect. I was not sure how to distract him. I did so much planning. I wanted it to be the best for Luke.

"Good morning, Luke, happy birthday," I whispered in his ear before he awoke. He smiled and turned around. I cuddled into his back.

66

"Oh, I need a few more minutes," he said as he turned into the pillow on the other side.

I was distracted by the details of the day. *Get him out of the house, keep him busy with his patients. Keep his mind on us doing something else.* Yikes! It was crazy enough it might just work. I let him sleep and watched the clock. We had to get moving. I kissed his shoulder.

"Luke, get up! You have a busy day!" I kissed his shoulder again. He didn't move. I got up and went to that side and pulled at his arm. He let go and turned the other way.

"Val, I just need like another fifteen minutes, okay?" He turned and brought the sheets with him.

I stood there and watched him and decided to go and take a shower. Moments later, he came into the shower with me. He tested the water, let it hit is face, and turned to me for a kiss as he drew me close.

"Thanks for the wishes."

I kissed him back and rubbed off the drops from his eyelashes. I made breakfast and got him out of the house as planned with a fifteen-minute delay. I watched for him to leave the farm and ran out behind him to gather all the things I needed for the day. I cooked feverishly. I thought of each detail of the decorations and where they should be placed. Pri came in and I had to have Frannie take her out. She could not hold a secret. It sometimes was hard to navigate around her.

The evening slowly approached. I was nervous. I wanted to wear the right outfit, make all his favorite dishes, and give him the surprise he deserved. He was under the impression that we would be alone and have a candle-lit dinner of steak and greens with his favorite dessert. I didn't listen to what he requested. I listened to what I wanted to give him.

The guests arrived and we hid in the living room. As he pulled up, I made sure I was in the kitchen, cooking and locking eyes as he came toward the house. The door slammed and he came over for his kiss. I led him to turn toward the living room and we all yelled, "Surprise!" He was not surprised. There was complete silence as he stood there in astonishment. His face was grim. He just stared at the crowd. I held onto his arm, thinking he was startled by the event. He pulled out of my grip and ran out of the house, got into his car, and drove away. I stood there with the crowd looking at me; whatever I had just done, I failed.

*　*　*　*　*

Cal walked home alone from mass that day. He thought long and hard to concentrate on moving forward to his next step. "I will hear the voices, I will hear the voices," he repeated to himself. He reflected at his time here in heaven. He had the time to spend with Madeline and Sheila. They made amends with each other and felt the love they didn't all have on Earth. He enjoyed the dinners, the times in the yard, the prayers they shared together, the long kiss she gave him when he came home. He loved it all. But it was time. He could hear it starting.

"Now, we have to go to the hospital now!" he heard the voices call out "Push, push!" He heard it and ran to the house.

"It's time. It's time. I am ready to go!"

Madeline, Sheila, and Ashley came around and were ready to go. They called over to Christopher and Dylan. They also came outside. They all met in the front yard and then he came over, the one Cal called "the big man." He was a vision of a man that you see in all the photos in statues in church. It was the man that said mass to them daily. It was Jesus.

"Cal, I am so proud that you have chosen to go back and serve on Earth. You will be entered into your new family and there will be a familiarity. Let's all gather around and give him our blessing. Say anything you need to say to him and release him from any unresolved business you all had together on Earth. Let him love and be loved."

Jesus blessed Cal and he kissed him, and Cal hugged everyone goodbye. There were no hard words that needed to be said. He felt at peace. Madeline gave him an extra kiss and touched his cheek and said, "Thank you for this."

He nodded, took a deep breath, and faded away. He awoke into the arms of Clarissa and John and would now start his new life as Mary Zavala.

Jesus let everyone sit around and just talk as a family, and he gave each one of them as much time as they needed alone with him to ask questions and get to know him on a personal level. This was Dylan and Christopher's first time. When he came over to Dylan, he asked about Valerie and how he was handling her being on Earth.

"It is okay, but hard. I want her to have a life. I just don't watch when she is with Luke. But it is okay. She will be here one day. I am enjoying my time with Peanut and meeting the family. I still have some things to work out with Christopher, but we will be okay. I am learning to forgive and let go."

"You have come a long way and have love in your heart. The anger is fading away. It will go away. Don't forget, we can have this time anytime you need it. Know you can always lean on me. Send me to your loved ones on Earth. You are doing all the right things and embracing time in heaven. I am proud of you," Jesus said as he touched Dylan's neck. He was blessed for the day. When Jesus left them, Christopher came over to Dylan to talk.

"Wow, that was an experience."

"Yeah, my first time too," Dylan replied and held Peanut tight.

"So, Dylan, I just want to let you know I worked out with Cal before he left that it is okay that I move in with Madeline and the girls. So we can be a family."

"I figured you would. Good for all of you, enjoy your time." Dylan gave him assurance and missed his roommate.

"Dylan, you are a gem. You truly are. We still need to talk. I really want to talk to you about Valerie." Christopher was nervous to ask but felt strong enough to talk about me so he could be with Madeline with no reservations.

"*Si, si*. Let's. In a few days, okay?" Dylan wanted to get it over with. He was sad that Cal left him and wanted to concentrate on praying for him. He also didn't want to hear about me with him just yet. But he wanted to face it and be over it.

"Thank you, Dylan, yes." Christopher embraced his girls and they waved as they entered into their home. Dylan went into the kitchen to make Peanut a new bottle. She grew a bit more since she had been with Dylan. He fed her and walked around the room. He saw me standing there in astonishment from Luke leaving the party and not knowing what to do.

"What happened, mi amor?" Dylan said out loud.

Peanut pointed and yelled out, "Momma!"

"Yes, that is your momma." He kissed her head and she touched his cheek to focus on his words.

"Your momma is sad today. She will be okay. Let us pray for her, Peanut. Pray for Momma. She needs us. Oh and Jesus, watch over her please? I want her to be okay."

He replied that he would.

*   *   *   *   *

I stood in amazement that the party I had planned was a disaster, and I didn't have any idea of where he went or even where he could go. Frannie gathered some of his colleagues and they separated to go on search for him. I asked the crowd to just move on with the party and not to worry; he was just frazzled. It was now a somber event, and I felt so foolish as I tried to play it off. Albina came over to comfort me.

"Not everyone can handle a surprise. He knows you meant well. Don't get upset."

I was fake smiling for the whole time and was starting to break my smile as the party went on and flopped at a rapid rate. *What did I do wrong here?* I leaned into Albina for a hug.

One by one, people picked up that Luke was not coming back, and if he did, he may not want to see them. They politely gave their "thank yous" with phony excuses to leave, and soon enough, it was just myself and Albina. Frannie called her.

"Everyone left. Any luck about where he could be?" Albina said. The search was off. Frannie came back and gave me a hug. I was sulking in a glass of wine at the island. I was still working on holding in my tears. More wine was poured.

"What did I do wrong?" I said, and then the breakdown occurred. Frannie and Albina consoled me but didn't have much to say. No one could understand what went wrong here. Frannie texted Luke again that the party was over and that I was upset but had nothing but the best intentions for the party.

We moved to the couch and opened another bottle of wine. I cried and they were amazing to hold me. Pri came in with Bingo and also came to hang out on the couch with us.

"Should I go get the good tequila?" Frannie asked as she held me close and kissed my head.

"No, no. Wine is fine. Is he ever going to talk to me again? Will I ever see him again? What happened?" I sulked further into Frannie and Albina poured more wine.

"I don't know, love, I don't know. Maybe he just doesn't like attention? What did he think you were doing tonight?"

"He thought we were going to have an intimate dinner alone. He never had a birthday party. He didn't grow up with a family. He was in foster homes, tossed around. I just thought that everyone should have a surprise party at least once in their life."

"Well, you came from a good place. Don't be upset. He knows it is from your heart, but maybe you should have read that he is in his sixties and never had a birthday party. Maybe there are some scars there."

"You're right, I just wasn't paying attention. He was so distant this morning. I didn't read it. Damn it! I feel so foolish!"

"Stop it, stop it, stop it. You are not foolish. He will be back, love, he will be back."

I cried some more. More wine was poured, and after tears were cleared up, Frannie took the ladies home and I sulked on the couch alone. I fell asleep with my wine glass in hand and my leg hanging off the couch and my head in the side pillow. The door slammed and I sat up immediately. Luke appeared. He stood at the edge of the kitchen right where the carpet started for the living room. He looked at me. He was angry. I sat up and just looked at him with mascara all down my face.

"I don't like surprises, Val," he said.

"Luke, I didn't know. I just didn't. I wanted to do something nice for you. You told me that you never had a birthday party. That hurt my feelings. I just wanted you to have that."

He puffed and walked outside onto the deck. I followed. We started to walk, and we walked toward the back of the farm past the rose patch and where a trail leads to a secluded bench. We sat down and let the moonlight guide the way. It was dark and I could see him through shadows.

He was cold. He was closed off. He was angry.

"Val, I just wanted a night alone with you. That is all I wanted and asked for. Why must you go and do something I didn't ask for?" His delivery was robotic and he looked straight ahead as I was hanging on him and begging for some affection.

"Luke, Luke. I just want to do something nice for you. I love you. I want to express that to you. I want to make up for the bad times you had. How can I break this wall and understand? I just want to be here for you."

He took a deep breath and readjusted his body language. It was asking me to give him space. It pushed me to my own spot on the bench.

"You can't change the past. You can't change me. You can't take away my pain. So stop. Stop thinking that you can or will be able to. I just wanted to be alone with you."

"Well, we are alone now, and you are pushing me away. I don't understand, Luke, I just don't."

"Val, I'm not opening that door right now. I am just not. Please don't ask me too. I had a horrible childhood. I was abused, run through foster families, treated like crap, at most. I was never acknowledged on my birthday as a child and when I was on my own. When I was married, I just asked for it to go away. I am sick of being used. I just want it to all go away. So please, if I ask for something like this, can you just grant my wish? I don't think I ask for much from you, Val."

"Luke, I didn't mean any harm. I could never use you. Let me take away your pain. No more surprises." Daringly enough, I went back to be closer to him. He still didn't accept it. This hurt was deep.

"You aren't using me, Val? You wanted this party, not me. It was for you, not me. You aren't using me to fill the void now that Dylan isn't around?"

"Luke, that is unfair. It is my understanding that the feelings between us are mutual. Do you not feel the same way? I can't believe you are saying this. How horrible. I want to give you everything that I can give. I want to take care of you. I want to love you. I do love you. My husband died. I can't change that. You know that and understand that. You needed me, I gave myself to you, and now you think I am using you for giving you a party? Thanks, Luke." I got up and walked toward the house. I was so upset. *How did I misread this situation? How did I misread our relationship? Why? Because I am not misreading this. This is anger speaking, not Luke. This is fear speaking, not Luke.* I went back to him as he sat there building up the wall to keep me out.

"I know that you are hurt. I know that there is pain that you have hidden deep within. I am not giving up on you. I am not giving up on us. We both have a past that doesn't go away. But we have a future, and you asked to be a part of mine. So I will not apologize for wanting to do something nice for you. So deal with being loved, because it can be pretty amazing. I learned so much from having Dylan as a husband. How to accept and give love. I have been given this gift to give it to you. So learn to love it, because it is not going to stop." I was in his face, waving my finger in between his eyes. Then I turned around and left him sitting there.

*   *   *   *   *

Marisol got her business degree from Duke University and decided to do some traveling before returning to the farm. I was at the age that I could start thinking of what I wanted to do with retiring, although I don't believe I could ever stop doing something for the farm or stop working altogether. Luke had decided to retire full-time, but since we lived on the farm, he dedicated himself to tending to our flock.

When Marisol came home, we decided it was best for her to take the guesthouse. There was no need for her to move back in with us as she should have her own space. She chose to stay on the farm and help out. We slowly worked on her taking over my businesses. I taught and guided her, then when she was comfortable enough, she would be able to go full-time and I could back off.

Luke and I spent the afternoons walking the entire property, and as we hit the rose patch, we stopped to say a prayer. I never stopped feeling them with me. I was lucky that Luke was so understanding and loving toward my past. I learned to be understanding about his and respect his privacy on the matter. I continued to let him know that I was always going to be there for him. We held early evenings on the porch with tequila and snacks. Sometimes, Frannie and Albina came over.

Marisol was still figuring out her place as a young twenty-something. She was dating and still not ready to make a commitment to anyone. We were so opposite in that direction. I was forever seeking someone permanent, and she was not interested. These are things that separated us. We sat on the porch, and when a car pulled up, we took bets on which guy was lucky enough to take her out that evening.

"Dylan would have a heart attack if he saw this show every night," Frannie said. We were all thinking it. I was so jealous of her confidence that she didn't need a man to complete her. When I was her age, that was all I thought of. The truck pulled up and they all threw out names of the ones they knew and then descriptions and nicknames of the ones they didn't.

"Michael," I said as I recognized the car from when he used to come and visit. This was his updated truck. He came out and came over to open the front door for Marisol, and she insisted to come over and say hello to the paparazzi across the way. We waved to welcome the homecoming.

"Hello!" he waved and said loudly.

They came up to the porch, and Frannie poured some tequila for them to share with us.

"Marisol, this is your father's secret stash."

"Oh, cool. He did love his afternoon tequila. Thank you, Frannie." She introduced Michael to everyone and left me for last. "You remember my mom, right, Michael?"

I got up to shake his hand. He was exactly what I expected. I was so proud of Marisol for seeing him in this capacity years ago. He fell into his own. His body was no longer awkward and he had become very handsome. His personality was no longer geeky. He held a very prestigious job at an investment firm and worked toward a few business ventures of his own. He still gawked over Marisol. He was also polite and kissed my hand as I held it out for him to shake. They sat and enjoyed a cocktail with us.

"So Michael, where are you taking Marisol this evening?" Frannie asked intrusively.

"We are going into the city and I am taking her to the new steak house I heard so much about," he replied.

"That is lovely, very nice," I replied to hopefully shut Frannie up. She was always very sarcastic and not afraid to barge into your business. I didn't want them to feel uncomfortable.

* * * * *

Dylan sat on the front porch once Peanut went to sleep. Christopher waited for him as he looked out the window and came over and sat in his lawn chair.

"Hey, Dylan, how are you?"

"I am good. How are things going with the girls? Everyone getting along?"

"Yes, oh, I could not be happier. It is better than imagined. I am so blessed. I never thought I could say that. Heaven is amazing."

"It is, it is indeed."

"So how are you doing? I feel as if I have had such an amazing time here, and I don't know you that well. I feel as if you are hesitant, not enjoying it up here as much as I am. There is no judgment. We are all on our own timeframe. I just want to see what I can do for you. You did so much for me on Earth and gave me so much here. I just feel as if you have so much more spirit within you? Does that make sense?"

"Ah, *si*, I am good. I am so enjoying the love up here, I really am. I am able to spend time with my daughter I never thought I would see again. I am upset I took away my life. I shouldn't have done that. I was angry and stupid. I was jealous. It ruined me. I was never ready to leave my family, leave Valerie. I am in penitence. I am so grateful that Jesus let me be here to take care of Peanut. But I have to take this pain and use it for someone who is not strong enough. I wasn't strong enough. I will get past this. I will see Valerie again. She is in my heart. So yes, it is hard. It is a struggle. But I will not give up. I believe. I hope that makes sense."

"It does. Valerie made me feel so special on my last days. I am so grateful for her. You have a heart of gold to be where you are and still care for her and not be mad. You know, she didn't know I was there that night. I didn't know you were there that night."

"I see that now. I just wanted to escape out of anger. I didn't want to leave her. It was not the right decision. I bet you know that wasn't right. Will you forgive me?"

"I have learned so much about forgiveness since I have been here. I forgive and I love what you have become to me. I wish you could forgive yourself. None of us are perfect."

"*Si, si*, I know. I am working on it. I am enjoying Peanut. I am just having such a time missing Valerie. I really am."

"She loves you. She never stopped. She let me know that. She loved you before she knew you. She thought it was me, but it was you. It always was. It held us from ever being together. So I hope that you understand that."

"I do. I am still processing it all. It is all good. I will feel better when she is here. I am not forcing her to get here anytime sooner than when she needs to be. I just mourn her. I really do. But it will all be okay. God is good."

"God is good. It took me a lifetime to find Madeline again. I am so grateful that Valerie led me back to her. Don't waste a lifetime again. Make peace so when she gets here, she can be with you and you both can resolve."

"Thank you, Christopher, I will do that. I will work through this. Thank you for your blessing." They embraced and Christopher went back to Madeline as a giggly teenager. Dylan sat and listened to them. "I still miss you, Valerie. I still do," he said, not remembering the echo could be heard.

*   *   *   *   *

My phone rang one morning as Luke and I decided to stay in bed late that morning for obvious reasons. I could not reach to grab it, and Luke grabbed it for me.

"It's Olivia?" he said with a smirk, not sure what that could mean.

"Olivia!" I screamed and grabbed it from his hand.

"Hello! Olivia! How are you?"

"Hello, Momma Valerie, how are you?"

"I am so good. What a pleasant surprise!" We spoke, but not as often as I would like. We hadn't seen each other in some time. She came over every few years for Christmas to John's. But she had a hard time returning to the farm.

"Valerie, I wanted to let you know. I am getting married! I want you to walk me down the aisle. I want everyone to come down to Mexico for the wedding. Please say yes, it would mean so much to me."

I was so elated with pleasure. Dylan would have loved this moment. *Oh, Dylan, how I wish you were here right now.*

"I am, *mi amor*, I am," I heard his voice in my head.

"Absolutely! Yes! Oh, Olivia, I am so blessed that you called me! I am so blessed to be a part of your life. Yes!"

*   *   *   *   *

Dylan played with Peanut in the backyard. She looked up and pointed. "Momma!"

"Yes, Peanut, that is Momma. She is happy. Let's send her love to be happy." Peanut threw out a kiss. I felt it.

*   *   *   *   *

Pri was becoming a little harder to handle over the past few years. She was demanding more and more of Luke's attention each time she saw me with him. He was a saint to hold tea parties with her, and hugs that she demanded became longer. I tried to discipline her, but her anger toward me was becoming strong as she did not understand relationships and struggled with understanding my relationship with Luke. Frannie shielded her as much as possible, and we tried our hardest to not show affection when she was around. It was starting to put a strain on us.

"Val, don't take this the wrong way, please. Pri is in her early thirties and still walking around with a stuffed animal. She has no friends of her own. I know, you will say that she loves the animals, but what is going to happen to her when you are gone? When Frannie is gone? John and Clarissa will not want to attend to Pri as she can be an unpredictable child herself. It's not fair to them. I can tell you for sure that Marisol is too busy chasing after young men to attend to her. Did you ever think about putting her in a group home or sending her to a place during the day to interact with others? I don't want to tell you what to do, but I also can't do this all day every day. I want to be spending all that time with you. I'm an old man! We have a late start here. I don't want to waste time."

"Oh, this is when I struggle with her. Oh, Pri, I feel like a horrible mother to you. I don't know what to do, Luke, I tried that before and she threw a tantrum that I had to come back and pick her up. It was horrible. Dylan was so upset as we always just wanted the best for her. It is so hard."

Luke came over to console me as I watched her out the window playing with Bingo on the swings. It broke my heart to watch her. Frannie said "Don't let it bother you, she is not fazed by it. She has the love of God in her heart." And I still cried. This was not fair to Luke nor to her. She needed to find her next home.

"There is a farm about thirty miles down that handles adults like her where she can live and work with the animals. I think when we go to Mexico, we should think about stopping to check it out?" He pulled up the website on his phone and the place looked lovely. We called and made an appointment.

The next week, we packed up and went on the long ride down to Mexico. I didn't think much about it until we got in the car. *This trip might be harder for me than I thought.* I remember snapping John, Olivia, and Pri in their seatbelts as they giggled and held their snacks. I remembered singing songs as we drove down the long lonely road. I remembered the truck we gave away as a parting gift that took away my baby in a red bag. I remembered the ring Dylan gave me from the girls. I remembered the stack of bills Dylan left on the dresser to get them to quiet down and go to sleep. I remember the look on Lydia's face when she kicked me. The look on her face when I came in to hug her as she gave us back the kids and said her final goodbye.

I drifted into that space that I had put away so many years ago. I held my wrist to my chest that felt warm from my body heat that used to be Dylan's, and I went into my chant again in my head as my lips moved. "Dylan, Dylan, Dylan." Luke saw me in my phase and reached over to me as the wind was strong with all the windows open and the speed pushed it harder into my face.

"How you doing, lady? Are you okay? You are drifting off somewhere." Frannie reached her hand over as she knew the pain I was bringing back up. Luke did not know the story.

"This is a hard memory, Valerie. You are a strong woman to come back here and do this for Olivia." She squeezed my shoulder and then sat back into the seat.

"Val, are you okay? What happened? Did I miss something?" Luke asked concerned. Dylan and I never told our story outside of the family. The kids never knew about Peanut. I only told Marisol because I made the mistake of bringing it up that day she came home from her visit with Christopher. Now Luke was in the dark, as he calls it, another "Zavala oops you found that one out?" moment. I turned to him and smiled as I swallowed my fears and anxiety.

"It's a lot, Luke, can we just talk about it later. I want this to be a happy trip. I am just worried about Pri and visiting this place." I smiled and touched his hand on his knee.

"Hey, Val?"

"Yes, Luke?"

"You are a shitty liar."

"Thanks, I will work on that."

He leaned in to kiss me. I went back to having the wind push my face as I held it to the window in case tears came. I did not want him to see them. After some time, we arrived at the farm. Pri was with John and Clarissa to help with Mary and distract each other for the long car ride. We wanted to check it out for ourselves before we let her see it.

"This place is nice. Wow, you can feel the calmness in the air," Frannie said as she got out of the car and stood a few feet away in a stance with her arms open wide and her eyes closed to embrace the land. We met with the directors and the staff who were all pleasant and warming. The rooms were clean, and the young adults that lived there seemed calm and happy. The farm had animals, and the daily routine switched around every few weeks so that they all could learn something new and not get stuck. Everyone was pleased with the accommodations.

Luke and I took some time alone to continue a walk around and discuss the options. He held his arm over my back and we held hands as I walked leaning into him as we did each afternoon around our farm.

"What are you thinking, Val?" he asked, hoping that the decision could be easy for me. I didn't answer right away and listened to the land, the wind. I was listening for Dylan. I didn't hear anything yet.

"I don't know, I don't know. This is a great place. For sure it is a great place. I am just waiting to feel something. I want to rest on it. I want to take this trip to think on it."

"Val, I am not Dylan nor her parent. This is a great place and not too far away. We can come and spend a few days here as often as you like to see her. I think it is good for her and for you. You spend so much time worrying about her. Don't wait until she is forced to be in a place where she has no decision on it because you are not around anymore. Sad to say, we need to start thinking about these things, Val. I think Dylan wants this for her, I really do. But it is your choice, Val, and I will respect what you want to do."

"Thanks, Luke, I know, I know. I don't want to hold her back. It is just a hard decision. I just want to think about it. I will know on this trip, I know it."

He gave me a kiss and we went back to Frannie and Albina, and Marisol stood taking selfies to post to her Instagram.

"I like it, Valerie, I really do," Frannie said and gave me a shake to hope that I was not dragging my feet on this one.

"I am going to think about it. I think this is a great idea. I just want to think about it for a few days."

"Are you waiting for Dylan to tell you it is okay?" Frannie said, and I looked away as I thought he had come to me right now and just said yes or no.

Dylan, where are you? I can't make hard decisions without you. I had no sign from him. "Yes," I said with distress in my answer. She gave me a hug and we all got into the car and drove away.

*   *   *   *   *

Dylan was able to hold Peanut's hand to mass as now she was big enough to walk and talk a bit. She was equivalent to a three-year-old. In heaven, she was progressing at her leisure. You could do that there. She held Dylan's hand and a small stuffed animal that looked like a dog. It looked like Bingo; she called him Lucky. Peanut's hair had wild curls as it had the same texture of Dylan's and my lighter brown locks.

"She gets those curls from me, you know!" Madeline said as she walked behind them.

Dylan laughed. "I bet she does." In the moment, all he wanted to do was be as close to her as possible, so he picked her up and carried her the rest of the way. He needed to hold her as the memory of Mexico was coming to his head and he felt horrible of the position he put myself and Peanut in. He was becoming upset as they entered into the church, and Peanut held onto his neck; and when they sat down, she put her head into his chest and played with his cross.

"Don't be sad, Daddy," she whispered into him, and he smiled as he kissed her forehead.

*   *   *   *   *

Dylan and I were very much in love. When I arrived in Texas, before Texas, we acted on it almost daily. I knew that I wanted to marry him. Our family situation and dynamic was overwhelming. *It will be soon.* I just knew it.

I wasn't so strict with our birth control routine. I suspected that I was pregnant about two months prior to our trip to Mexico but dismissed the first month just out of stress and the overwhelming feeling of the sudden move to Texas. By the end of the second month, I knew. I was afraid to tell Dylan. I had no one to tell that I trusted. One afternoon, I went into town to take a break before picking up the kids from school. I snuck into the bathroom of Walmart and took the pregnancy test I just bought. It was there—pregnant.

I had so many emotions running through my mind. *What will I do? Will Dylan and I get married? Does this seem like a trap? I don't want to have a baby out of wedlock. It was not what I had planned for.* I had a sudden love for this baby and could feel it in me. I went to a cute baby store that customized in all the adorable preppy things I loved so much. I wandered around the store to see what my intuition gravitated toward.

"Baby, who are you? What are you? I already love you so much," I said to my abdomen. Then I walked to a pink gingham bed set. There I knew it was going to be a girl. I purchased the set and a few dresses to match that were irresistible. I purchased a boy's set as well, just in case. But I knew it was going to be a girl. I decided to tell Dylan that night after dinner, after he had a glass of wine or maybe a tequila; after he was tired and just wanted to be with no one other than me; after I had pleased him and made him smile before bed. I had it all planned out.

I wanted a proposal, I wanted to start our family. I wanted so much so fast. It wasn't in my timeframe, it was in God's timeframe. I kept telling God what I wanted. I didn't listen to what he wanted for me.

When we came home that day, I found out we were heading to Mexico. I placed all the clothing in the attic and decided to wait until we got back. I thought to myself that a few more days couldn't hurt. It could've been a good distraction as we would be upset until they came back. I should have told him sooner.

"Dylan and Peanut, will you forgive me? Would it make a difference?" I don't know. I never touched the clothes again. I never picked out a name for her. I hoped that she would one day be able to understand how much I missed her and wanted her in my life. "I love you, Peanut," I said out loud as I prayed daily in the rose patch. *Oh, the secrets we keep.*

We drove straight through and got to the border. The line was not as long as the last time I was here.

"Ladies, I think we can make it through in about an hour. Do you want to stop or should we just keep going?"

"Keep going," I said before anyone could respond. I was anxious to get through this. The anticipation grew and I was determined to make it past this point. I texted Olivia that we were at the border. She sent back a thumbs up.

*   *   *   *   *

Dylan sat at mass and he lost his concentration to look at Peanut and run his hand through her crazy curls. Each time, Madeline looked over and sent out a giggle because Peanut was just so cute. When mass was over, Lydia and Miguel came to greet them as they had not seen Peanut so grown up. Dylan invited them over for some coffee and cake.

*   *   *   *   *

As we neared the border, my heart continued to race and the car was silent.

"Val, I am kind of worried about you. Are you okay? I don't like to see you like this. What happened, Val?"

I took a deep breath, and as we passed through and gave our passports, I saw Olivia on the other side with a bouquet of flowers and was able to break the conversation. I got out of the car which alarmed Luke, but he saw Olivia and understood. I ran to her and he drove behind me. Frannie and the ladies held hands, and when they all got close enough, they got out of the car in time to watch me run into Olivia's arms. I held her so tight.

I remembered Dylan down on one knee with the red string ring the girls made for me. I remembered the look on his face of worry. He did not know how to move on if I said no, if he let me walk away that day; the understanding that if he went alone to the house, he may not be returning.

*   *   *   *   *

Dylan felt the anxiety hit him as he sat with Lydia and Miguel at the kitchen table and stood up to go and look out the window. I hugged Olivia and she hugged me back. Dylan touched the window as he could see us. Lydia and Miguel walked behind him as they could see us too.

"Olivia." Lydia let out a cry for her and Miguel consoled her. "She is so beautiful," Lydia said and turned to Miguel to weep in his chest.

Dylan stood with his finger on the window and watched us, trying to feel what that bond at that moment felt like.

"You are so beautiful, Olivia, I am so excited to be here for you. Your mother would have been so proud of you. Dylan would have been so proud of you."

We shed tears and she moved on to hug the others. I looked around as I felt someone watching me. I looked around and the wind picked up.

"Momma!" Peanut screamed from upstairs as she was watching from her bedroom window also. Dylan smiled and ran up to see her. He picked her up and sat at the window with Peanut on his lap.

"Yes, Peanut, that is Momma and your sister, Olivia. Olivia is getting married, did you know that?"

She shook her head no and he leaned back to continue to watch us. I looked up and waved as I knew he could see me.

"Oh, *mi amor*, how much I miss you." Dylan blew a kiss and I felt it.

*   *   *   *   *

We drove to the house, the same house that I was beaten in. It had changed. I rode with Olivia and we held hands, and she told me all about her fiancé. She was so excited and could not wait to introduce us all. We arrived at the house that was completely renovated, and she lived there for now with Pedro as he was up there in years and she wanted to watch over him. They moved close by to care for him. Pedro came out when we pulled up to the house as the sun was setting.

"Greetings," he said and gave us all hugs. I never saw him with a smile before. He was quite dashing when he allowed himself to be. The anger was gone; the past was over. We were here for a special celebration. We embraced.

"Ms. Valerie, so nice to see you again. You are lovely as always. Olivia is very happy that you came."

"Thank you, Pedro, we are very happy to be here. Please, come and meet my boyfriend, Luke." I brought him over to the car and they started shaking hands and then embraced.

"Valerie, aren't you a little old to have a boyfriend? This is a man!" he said, and we chuckled as he slapped Luke on the back. It was nice to start a relationship with Pedro.

Frannie knew her way around as this was, once upon a time, her house. She took Albina on a walk, and Olivia brought us over to meet her fiancé, Enrique. He was so handsome, like a young Clark Kent. He was charming and very polite. He welcomed us with open arms and double kisses as if he was French.

Enrique was American, born and raised in Louisiana where his family started a business that manufactured in Mexico. That is where he came to work and met Olivia at an outside lounge one evening. We sat on the porch and drank tequila as Enrique told us the story.

"She was with her friends at this little place in town. The salsa music was playing. The girls were getting tipsy. I was in a suit as I had a business meeting but managed to take off my tie and jacket after a few tequilas. She kept looking over as they danced, and I was distracted by her beauty. I looked over as well and sent them another round of tequilas. They cheered up to us and didn't come over. I was like, 'Come on, I bought you drinks and no thank you?' She still looked over, I still looked over. My colleague asked me to just go over already, and after a few more drinks, we did. She taunted me as she danced. Then soon enough, she came over to dance with me. I held her waist, she held her hands on my neck, and we just danced with no words for the rest of the night.

"When the bar was closed, she kissed my cheek and walked away. She walked away! This strong confident woman stole my heart and I became a school boy chasing after her in the parking lot until she turned around and finally kissed me. I drove her home and realized I didn't even know her name! I was so into her, I didn't even get her name. How silly and foolish I was as I laughed in my empty hotel room. Oh, I could not sleep.

"The next day, I went to pick up some flowers and went back to her house, and she knew I did not know her name. She taunted me at the door that she would not open it until I said her name. She gave me hints, and after she said 'Newton-John,' I knew it was Olivia. And with that, she opened the door and gave me a kiss. We have not been apart since!"

He was smiling and stood to tell the story, and as he was done, he went and sat himself next to Olivia who hung on his words and gazed at his handsome chiseled smile.

Pri went up to sit a bit uncomfortably too close to Enrique, and he was not really in an understanding of Pri's setbacks. "Did you meet Bingo?" she said to Enrique just as he finished his story, and it took away the mood. I felt embarrassed as it was stealing their limelight. I went to grab Pri and bring her close to me on the other side of the deck. Frannie cringed at me, and I again felt like the "bad mom."

"No, no. It's okay, Valerie, Mom. She can stay." Olivia reached out for Pri who went running back to them, and they had a side conversation as the awkwardness resonated within me.

Luke pulled me closer as he knew I was embarrassed. Pedro poured more drinks and handed out some Pigs in a Blanket. Pedro sat by us and asked about Pri.

"She is special. I don't know what to say." I held onto Luke in embarrassment and a bit of anger about it. Pedro was hurt by watching her and walked away from us as he paced the backyard and kicked dirt in frustration. I watched him and held in a bit of anger. Luke did not understand what was going on between us. He felt a Zavala secret being released.

"Val, what's going on here?" Luke asked. I kept watch on Pedro, and Olivia was now taking notice of his absence and looked to also watch him and then looked at me.

She said to me from across the porch in a signal, "What happened?"

I just gave her a shrugged back.

She got up and went to talk to Pedro and Enrique, had Bingo on his lap, and was giving Pri a show.

"Valerie?" Luke whispered back into my ear. "What is going on?"

I went to answer him, but I couldn't. I slapped his leg and caressed it and smiled at him and gave him a kiss. "Some doors are hard to open for me too, Luke," I said and got up to walk for a bit in the other direction. Frannie went after me. The rest sat there, not really understanding what was going on.

"Frannie, I don't want tears, and I don't want to take this moment away from Olivia. I just don't so I am just gathering myself together and pushing my anger aside. He knows it is his fault for not getting her help. He has no idea how hard it was to raise her. I just want to do the right thing. That is all."

"Valerie, honey. You are doing the right thing. I think sending her to that farm is the perfect place. Albina and I have been talking about retiring also. I am old! I am almost ninety! I can't keep up anymore, and she needs to move on. Listen to Luke, don't wait for Dylan. He trusts that you will do the right thing. Now go and tell Pedro that you are sending her to live on that farm and it will all be okay. *Go!*"

She was right. I needed to make this okay, so I did as she asked. I put on a smile and waved over to Olivia and Pedro, and they stood in astonishment as they were expecting me to blow up on them.

"Pedro, don't be upset. It is old news. Look at her. She is happy. So very happy. She doesn't know any better. It has been a journey, for sure a hard journey, and I must think about what is best for her future. We went today to visit a farm that takes care of people in her situation. She can live there with people like her. I am getting old, Frannie is super old. The kids need their own life with their own kids. Marisol is in her self-absorbed phase. But will she want to care for her sister forever? It is a full-time job to care for a grown child.

"Don't get me wrong. I am not complaining at all. I love her with all my heart, so I must do this for her. So let's put this aside. Let's put all the anger and tension behind us and let's celebrate life and the wonderful union of Olivia and Enrique. That is what we came here for. For Love. Dylan, Miguel, Lydia, and Peanut would want that for her. I believe in that. I am sure they are all watching over us smiling."

Pedro smiled back and gave me a hug. "Peanut?" he asked.

I took a deep gulp and held in my tears. "Yes, Peanut. The baby I lost the last time I came to visit."

I held our heads together and he started grumble up tears. "Let it go, Pedro, be at peace and let it go." I held my hand firmly on his neck and he shook his head yes and we headed back to the group for some much needed tequila.

That night, we got ready for bed, and as Luke and I brushed our teeth, he asked again. "So what is going on, Val? I don't mean to be a dick, but what happened with Pedro today? What kept you so anxious on our way here? I feel like I am really out of the loop and it is kind of uncomfortable."

He was right. There was too much history, and it was unfair for him to not know it. I nodded my head as I was brushing and spat out paste. "I will tell you everything. Let's get into bed." And so we did.

We got comfortable and Luke let me lay into him, and he held my hand from across my neck. I nuzzled into him as I had found all the right spots in him.

"Luke, this is hard, so bear with me. You know that we came to drop off the kids back to Lydia, then she got sick and gave us back Pri and John. Olivia stayed."

"Yes, dear. I know that part. Go on."

"So when they were here for a few years, they didn't go to school. It was prime time for Pri to get the much needed attention for her learning disabilities. They didn't do anything for her, so now she struggles. It is hard to see how much she needed that attention. Pedro didn't see it until today. So it hurts, but you are right. She should go to that home, and on the way back, let's take her there and sign the papers."

"Really, Val? That is so great. Really, it is. I am proud of you. You are making the right choice for her. But don't let this stop your story. I know that there is more."

"Damn it. All right, there is more. Yes, it was ugly. When we came here with the kids, they stole them from the car and Dylan and I went chasing after them. They beat us badly. I was pregnant and lost the baby. Where Dylan is buried, he planted that rose patch for our baby. We called her 'Peanut.' No one knows about the baby, but Frannie and now Marisol. Today, I told Pedro as it was him and Lydia who beat me the most. I had a miscarriage at a local hospital and we had to pay cash. It was horrible. I am sorry for not telling you, but you know us Zavalas, we love our secrets."

Luke kissed my forehead as I was trying to make light of the situation. He gave me another kiss. "Valerie, thank you for telling me your story. It means the world to me. You have no idea. I now know that you really do love me and care for me. You have no idea."

"Luke, I do love and care for you. I really do. I just want the best for you and to take care of you."

"Val, do you know how I know that is true and genuine?"

"No. Maybe because I have been showing you? Broke you down?"

He kissed my head again. "You know that Dylan was my best friend, right?"

"I didn't think of it like that, but yes. You are right, you guys were best friends."

"Well, when you got back from Mexico, Dylan told me the whole story. Everything. He was so upset about Peanut, and I helped him plant the roses. He swore me to never tell anyone, and I didn't. Years later, before he died, we were on the farm together going for a walk around as I was going to be watching over it when you guys went to get married, again. We were talking about you. He was so excited that you guys were going to get married again, and he was so happy that you took him back. It was the happiest I can remember him. You guys were flirty and just very cute.

"We stopped at the rose patch and he said a prayer to Peanut, asking her to watch over you guys. He took me by the shoulder as we stood there and told me that they never told the kids about Peanut and no one else other than Frannie. He told me that if anything ever happened to him, he wanted you to go and love someone else until you could be with him again. He said that his love was so strong for you that he would be able to hold on to that for as long as he needed too. He told me that he will be watching over and know that you truly loved someone if you were able to tell them that story and be able to bring them to Mexico. So, Valerie, Dylan is watching over us now and letting me know that you do love me while you are here on Earth, and I am truly blessed to be with you and have you in my arms right now. I love you, Valerie Zavala, I love you. I can't tell you how much this weekend means that you brought me here."

I turned around to lay on his chest and outline his shoulders with my finger. I smiled at him as he smiled back. It meant so much to know that Dylan approved of this gathering and he always knew who I was.

"I believe in you, Dr. Luke." We kissed and ended the night, utilizing the left and the right side of the bed.

The next morning, we were awakened by Pri standing over the bed on Luke's side as I was draped across him.

"Valerie, why are your clothes on the floor?" she said.

I still did not have my eyes open. "Pri, you can't just walk into someone's bedroom uninvited like that. Go back to your room!"

She ran back, and a few minutes later, she came back. Luke and I did not move much from the position we were in the first time.

"Luke, can we go on a date today?"

"Pri! I told you not to come in here unannounced! No, you cannot go on a date with Luke today. We have Olivia's wedding. Now it is too early to be awake, so please go back to bed!"

Frannie came over to the room as she heard me get stern and frustrated with Pri. Frannie took Pri back to her bed until it was an acceptable time to show their faces.

"Why is Valerie sleeping in bed with Dr. Luke?" she asked.

"Honey, that is Valerie's boyfriend. You ladies talked about that. She has sleepovers with him. She loves him, Pri, like she loved Dylan. Now come and cuddle with your grandma."

Pri was upset and uneasy as she really didn't understand how everyone was pairing off and she did not have a significant other. She still didn't understand that Luke and I were a couple and had been for years. She really needed to be somewhere with people like her. Our environment was starting to harm her. When Frannie dozed off, Pri found herself coming back into our room, and we were back at finishing business we started last night.

"Pri!" I screamed and grabbed to cover us with the sheets. "Pri, I told you that you are not invited in here unless you knock. What do you want?"

"Valerie, I don't understand why you stole my boyfriend from me. Why are you so mean?"

Here it was—my mean mother moment that I thought was taken care of. My daughter found me and my boyfriend having sex and she thought that he was her boyfriend. I felt like I should be on Jerry Springer.

Marisol and Frannie came running down the hallway and stood in the doorframe to try and alleviate the situation. Luke was frustrated.

I covered us and sat us back into the bed and asked everyone to gather around and sit. They did. Luke was frustrated and uncomfortable by this situation. It had to end here today. "Pri, I did not steal your boyfriend. Luke is my boyfriend and you must accept that. I told you that you could take him on walks and have hugs and tea parties, but that is it. You know that he lives with me and we have been together for some years now. This should not be a shock to you, Pri. Now listen to me. I want you to have a boyfriend and friends your age that are like you. Would you like that?"

"Yes, Momma Valerie, I want a boyfriend and friends."

"I know you do. I am glad that you do. I have been so selfish, Pri, I really have. I wanted you to stay with me on the farm and help me because you are so good at it. I wanted to have you close to me because you are such a good cuddler and an amazing daughter. I love you so much, Pri. Do you know that?"

At this point, Olivia has made her way to the room and took her spot on the bed. It reminded me of when I first came to Texas and how stunned I was as they all climbed into our bed. I felt it when Olivia came in. I had my family together again. It felt good. I knew that Dylan was watching over us. It felt good.

Albina came over and Frannie signaled her to come and sit with us. It was a true blessing to be so close and to see Frannie smile.

"Yes, Momma, I want that. I do!" She held Bingo and stood right in front of me at the side of the bed.

"Good, Pri, I am so happy to hear that. I have a friend who has a farm, and they desperately need someone like you to help and watch over the animals for them. How do you feel about going to help them? There are young men and woman just like you there and want to have a friend, maybe even a boyfriend. You are so special, Pri, and so beautiful. You have so much to offer. I think that you should be there and help them. What do you think, Pri?"

"What about you, Momma Valerie? Will you miss me?"

"Oh, of course, I will! But Pri, I will come and visit you, and you can come and visit us. What do you think?"

"I will come visit you too," Olivia said.

"Me too," said Marisol.

"Us too," said John and Clarissa as they walked in and grabbed a hug from Pri.

We all gave her the reassurance that this was the right thing, and I kept my focus on her as she started to give a look of doubt.

"Okay, Momma, I will go."

I went in to for a hug and she then pulled away to dance with Bingo and tell him about their new home. Frannie took her to her room to get dressed and I leaned back into Luke and the family all took a big deep breath. Olivia grabbed my leg and came in close to lay on me and give me a hug.

"Valerie?" she asked, and she laid into my stomach.

"Yes, love?"

"Remember when you first came to Texas and tucked us in? And I told you I didn't like you?"

"Yes, love, I do."

"Then Pri told me that she did and I felt stupid. When I was here with my mom before she died, she told me the best thing for Pri was to be with you. It was the smartest decision she ever made. I remembered that moment and was so jealous of you for having such a bond with her so quickly. And I didn't, so I was mad at you. But now I love you so much and am so grateful to have you in my life. I love you, Valerie. Thank you for being the best thing for our family."

Luke reached over to hold me closer and was touched by our conversation.

"I love you too, Olivia, and all of you kids. I always did from day one." They all leaned in and Mary came to my side to kiss my cheek.

"I love you, Grandma!" she screamed.

"I love you too, Mary. Don't call me Grandma!" We all laughed and hugged and parted ways to get ready for a wedding.

*   *   *   *   *

When Marisol was in her last year of elementary school, it was a very cold winter for us in Texas. We had to buy the kids winter coats as they never had experienced cold. It even snowed a bit once. You forget how the seasons change when you have lived here so long. It is kind of funny when they close school, because it is too cold and they don't have the heat to support the school. These are things I laugh about living here. *Oh, New York, you made me see the world in a "tough girl" light.*

It was cold, and Dylan did not wear a coat. I made him put on fleeces that he just took off once he got deep into the farm. I made him extra coffee to keep warm and switch out his usual breakfast for oatmeal to keep him hearty. But it was inevitable. The stubborn Latin in him did not give in. His hot blood went right into his head. He went back to his t-shirt on the farm out in the cold, working himself too hard. He always lived in his passion. Then it happened. The sneezes, the cold sweats, the dizziness. The six-foot-one man coming back to the house, asking me to check his head for a fever.

"I told you that you were going to get sick! It is thirty degrees. You can't walk around in a t-shirt."

"Do I have a fever?" he asked as his face was flush and his body was sweaty.

I went to find a new fleece for him as the others laid somewhere on the farm and could not be found. I made him take off his sweaty tee shirt and get straight into bed with Theraflu. He shook, through the hour he drifted off into a deep sleep that made his snore loud enough I could hear him downstairs. He had the flu. I was angry as he could have prevented this if he just took better care of himself. His stubbornness always got the best of him.

The kids came home from school and I asked them all to hush as he was asleep upstairs. They were in astonishment because he never got sick.

"Dad is sick? What, really?"

"Yes, John, really. See what happens when you don't listen to me? Now all of you go and get your homework started. I am putting dinner on now and I want you guys to be quiet and go to bed early. No one else in this house needs to get sick right now."

They all wanted to see the act of Dylan in bed snoring away and know what it looked like for him to be sick. I could not stop them from running up the stairs. I would be in the flu season for the next two months now as they tossed it back and forth to each other. I could not afford to have it as this was my motherly promotion. "Dylan!" I said to myself angry at his stubbornness. He snored, the kids stood at the doorway to watch, and he never came in the house during the day; He never naps. He hardly snores. It was better than a video game.

Dylan slept with his hand on his chest, hat still on. The blankets I made him wear he already tore off. He was not fazed by them standing there and talking about him so loudly. He was overworked, too tired, and defeated. Dylan had the flu. They found this exciting. I think it made him human to them, and not the superstar they always made him out to be.

I came up behind them and watched as I did not understand the astonishment, but it was sweet that they cared so much.

"Momma Valerie, I am going to make Dylan a sign to make him feel better," Pri said and ran into her room.

"I am going to get my baseball glove so when he wakes up, he will want to play catch," John said.

"I am going to make him cookies. Mom, can you help?" Marisol said.

"He doesn't need cookies, silly girl!" I messed up her hair and she laughed.

"All right, everyone, dinner in ten minutes so act fast and leave Dylan alone, please. He needs sleep, not stuff!" I went back downstairs to finish getting dinner ready. As the kids went into their rooms to prepare something for Dylan, Marisol went to sit next to him. She touched his hand on his chest and Dylan in a deep sleep awoke, startled as his REM was at its deepest state.

"I just wanted to give you love and hope you feel better," she said to him.

"Thanks, *mi amor*," he said back and closed his eyes again. A few minutes later, his snore was back to a high level.

I went back up to gather them for dinner and peeked my head in to see if Dylan was still sleeping and okay. He was back to his snore. His hat now on his face, I moved it off and went back down to share a meal with the kids.

We ate, the kids had dessert, I read bedtime stories, and tucked them each into their bed. I looked in on Dylan as he still didn't move from his comatose state. I cleaned up downstairs and came in to the bedroom, afraid to sleep next to him, to wake him up, or even contract whatever he had. I decided to wake him.

"Dyl, Dyl."

He opened his eyes, startled.

"Hey, babe, how are you feeling? I want you to take another Theraflu and some liquids. Will you please eat something?"

He took a few moments to swallow and realize he was parched. He needed time to process what time it was and the fact that he was sicker than he realized.

"Hey, yeah, some water would be good. Thanks, Valerie."

He attempted to sit up a bit more but was weak. I grabbed the water bottle on the night table and brought it to his lips. He was so pale and fragile.

"Let me make you something to eat, something small to build strength? I don't want you to take more medicine on an empty stomach."

He nodded. I touched his forehead and it was hot. I was starting to get nervous of how serious this could be. I went downstairs to make him soup and brought it up to him.

I fed him soup and Pri came in to watch. She sat patiently on the side of the bed and touched his ankle to console him as I fed his soup at his weak pace. She was calm and collected. It was so warming to have her there. After a few minutes, she went back to bed without a fight. Dylan smiled.

"She has such a warm heart," he said to me. He was starting to feel better.

"She does, she does." I smiled back, kept my concentration on him. It was hard to see him so weak. He ate and walked about to test out his strength. I hesitated to stay in the room with him that evening and excused myself to the couch.

"Wait, you are going to sleep downstairs?" he said as I grabbed my pillow and a blanket.

"Yeah, you are not well. I want you to sleep peacefully tonight. I don't want to bother you."

"Valerie, I haven't slept a night without you in years. I can't sleep soundly knowing you are downstairs."

"You slept well this afternoon. I think you will be okay." I grabbed my things and headed down the stairs.

"Valerie, please. I need you. I want you here with me. Please stay with me."

The kids all perched up in their beds to know what I decided to do. I stood at the top step and hesitated.

"Please, Valerie." He sat up and held out his hand, his voice weak and his face pale. *I'm his nurse and should stay close by? Ugh, I don't want to get sick too. But I don't want to sleep a night without him.* I went back into the bedroom and crawled into bed. He sank into his pillow and was back into his fast snore.

*　　*　　*　　*　　*

Olivia was so beautiful as she put on her wedding dress and let us be a part of this ceremony. She glowed.

"Momma Valerie, what do you think?" she said to me as she looked at me through the mirror. I was taken back by her beauty. Her hair up in braids and curls, her dress flowing in the wind. Her comfortability of the day, her assurance that Enrique was the best man for her. She held a small bouquet of flowers of a white array. She was so beautiful. I hoped that Dylan was watching.

I walked her down the aisle. They said their vows. We danced under tea lights, drank champagne, and enjoyed the laughs that day brought. Luke grabbed me and some champagne as we danced, and he moved us to a quite spot on the dance floor. He was dashing, his navy-blue tux was so perfect. His smile was, again, infectious. We danced, and he drew me closer.

"Valerie, thank you again for letting me into your world. I feel special."

"You are special, Luke, you are so special to me. Never forget that."

"I won't." He twirled me around. Soon, John came over to us and stole me from Luke's hold.

"Valerie, this is so awesome, isn't it?" John said to me as we slow-danced to a fast song I did not know the words too. I was so happy, I was giggling.

"Yes, John! This is so great. I am so happy for you and your family. Enjoy each moment. You are so successful with baseball and your family is beautiful. Enjoy it. We all have a short time here. Enjoy it. Your parents and Dylan want you to."

"Valerie, you and Dylan are my parents. I love you, we all love you. Thank you for taking us back from here years ago. Thank you for taking us here this weekend. We had the best upbringing thanks to you. Dylan was so lucky to meet you. He really was."

"Oh, no, thank Jesus. I was lucky to meet him. He truly saved me. He is my angel. I miss him every day."

"I do too. So, Valerie, my baseball contract is up soon. I want to start to take over the farm with Marisol. We have been talking about it for a bit and think it is time. You need to take off, travel more with Luke. Enjoy your life. You never took a break!"

"Ha-ha! Yes, I don't think I know how to. Yes, I admit defeat. I want to spend more time with Luke. Are you mad that I am sending Pri away? I feel conflicted on this."

"No, no way. She really needs it. It will be wonderful for her."

"Thanks, John, you are the new man of the house. I now hand the hat to you." I took a bow, and he held me and laughed. We had a wonderful moment together.

At that time, Clarissa, Mary, Marisol, and Luke came over and we danced together. It was a beautiful weekend. I hoped that Dylan was watching.

We said goodbyes as Olivia and Enrique became a family. We switched up the cars as Frannie and Albina wanted to travel a bit more in Mexico. I had the hard task of taking Pri to her new home. I was so nervous about this.

"She is going to be fine. Stop and relax!" Luke said to me as we got in the car. Pri was clueless. I replayed in my head when she came into our bedroom yesterday and wondered if she was getting worse. I think she was. *Is it her memory? Is it just a phase? Oh, I hope that I am doing the right thing.* She held her head out the window with Bingo in tow. I tried to calm my frustration, and Luke sensed it. He held my hand as he drove us back to the States.

Six hours later, we arrived at the home where Pri would spend the rest of her days. I had to play this off. Luke gave me a nod as he shifted into gear and turned off the car.

"Wow, Pri, this is such a cool farm. I bet they have lots of animals here. Isn't this cool?" Luke started off and gave me a wink as we all got out of the car. She opened the door and started to run to the gate. We were greeted by one of the directors.

"You must be Pri," she said as we walked up behind her.

"Yeah! I heard you need me? Can I see your animals?" She was pushing her way past the director and wanting to run into the farm to see the horses running around. She was escorted from us with one of the supervisors and we walked behind and spoke to the director.

"I think she has been slipping the past few months, and I am the horrible mom that is just seeing it now."

"Well, she will get evaluated while she is here, and we have the best team of doctors on staff. Look at her, she is so happy."

Pri was introduced to some of the other young adults staying there and was already hugging them. She was smiling. The director took us to where her room was. It was a nice corner view of the farm. She will be able to look out and enjoy the animals anytime she wanted to. We signed the paperwork, went to buy her all the goods she needed for her room, and came back to her enjoying dinner with her new friends. It was best to leave her there. If she came home, it would be a struggle to bring her back. We went over to say our good-byes and let the staff take her from there.

"Hi, Pri!" I said as Luke and I grabbed chairs to sit behind her. I combed her hair with my fingers.

"Momma, stop playing with my hair in front of my friends!" She was a little bossy, but it felt good that she was comfortable and enjoying her popularity. I met the group at her table and they all got along. All had smiles on their faces and were well-adjusted. I sat back and, in my head, called for Dylan to give me the sign that it was okay. I heard nothing but silence. Luke leaned in and let me know it was time to go.

"Come and give me a hug. I am going to leave you here with your friends. They need you. I will be back next week to check on you. How does that sound?"

"Momma Valerie, I love it here. Thank you for letting me help them. Yes, they need me." She gave me a huge hug and we walked out as I left Priscilla Zavala on her own to become the adult she never wanted to be.

*　*　*　*　*

When Madeline and Cal first got married, they loved to entertain with family and friends. Their BBQs were big during the summers. Madeline always loved to grill up some steaks and make a bunt cake. They always made sure the drinks were flowing.

Cal was dashing. She did her best to not gawk at him and let it get to his head. But she did watch as others did gawk at him, and he enjoyed it. Madeline's sister, Carrie, was not shy about flirting with Cal. He was not shy about flirting back.

It started on the beach when they all met together. He could have had his pick, but he chose Madeline. Some days, Madeline questioned herself as to why. But as she won at this game of Cal, she trusted that he picked her because his feelings were stronger for her. She forever questioned it.

Carrie was also a very good-looking woman. She had a much stronger personality than Madeline, which made Madeline insecure. Madeline was always on eggshells each time Carrie came over. Cal smiled as she let herself in after a quick knock. Madeline felt chills down her spine but put on a good show in front of the crowd. They always struggled with power between the sisters. Madeline fell short to Carrie on most occasions. Carrie was not afraid to let go of her prey.

Carrie loved to come in like a hurricane, in a fabulous dress that she embellished from a plain original she bought in town. Her lipstick, eyelashes, and pearls always perfectly intact. When she entered a room, she fixated herself next to the most handsome man there. In Madeline's house, Carrie was fixated on Cal. Carrie never married. I feel as if she liked to perform this dance on the edge that fulfilled her. I was sad for Aunt Carrie.

The party was set, some friends over for a Friday night snowstorm party, drinks, and cards. Probably mostly drinks. Everyone came at the appointed timeframe, but Carrie of course came late to make an entrance, just as everyone was on their second, possible third drink. She walked in a bit tipsy herself and leaned on Cal to test the waters of his level of letting his guard down.

"Oh, Cal, can you help me with this wet coat? I am having a hard time here," she said as she looked him in the eye.

He came running over to her and obliged. Madeline went into the kitchen to replenish her drink and let out a silent scream. Carrie had on a tight top and big skirt during this snow storm. As her coat came off, she took a hold of Cal's beer and drank straight from the bottle—a big swig. When she finished his bottle, she handed it back to him and demanded another. Cal went into the kitchen to replenish their drinks and found Madeline angry at the sink. He came behind her as she pushed him off and went outside to the party. He was not sure what he had done wrong.

The card game got to become a round of shots and cigarettes, giggles, and everyone forgetting that the snow outside was piling up. Someone insisted to capture the moment with the photo. Carrie moved her way to snuggle next to Cal as Madeline was shoved to the other side of the party. She snuggled into him as the flash went off—Madeline looked down in disappointment and Carrie was all smiles on Cal's side before he even knew what happened.

The party ended, everyone walked home in the snow, and Madeline stormed up the stairs into the bedroom without even touching what needed to be cleaned up. Cal started to pick up the mess and was not understanding what happened between himself and Madeline. Nothing had ever happened between Carrie and him; his love for Madeline was too strong. She lost trust in him, maybe she never loved him at all. Maybe she was not satisfied with what they had. Maybe she was always wanting more and thought Cal could give it to her. The strain on their relationship started that night. Cal never understood why.

When they got a copy of the photos from that night, there it was—the picture of Carrie on Cal's shoulder as her head turned to him. Cal was stunned she came in so close, and he was asking her politely to back off. But all that came out in the photo was his head turned into hers and it looked as if they were about to kiss. Cal felt like he now understood why Madeline was so cold. He asked that Carrie never come to their home again. She didn't. Madeline and Carrie did not speak much after that time. Cal continued to work on getting back into Madeline's good graces.

*   *   *   *   *

The door slammed earlier than usual that morning and Luke opened his eyes wide and exclaimed, "Doesn't anyone ever knock in this place?"

I chuckled into his shoulder as the entrance walked right up the stairs into our bedroom. It was, of course, Frannie.

"Frannie! Really? Like, do you ever knock? Do you have any boundaries?" Luke screamed as he was not going to win this war.

"No," she said.

"Did she do this when Dylan was here?" he asked me.

We both answered back, "Yes."

Frannie sat on my side of the bed as he held the covers up as close to our chins as possible. She slapped my leg as she did most times when she had something important to discuss. Frannie got herself comfortable and pushed myself and Luke over, and he sighed.

"Okay, so I need to tell you something. Albina is not doing so well, and I am also an old lady. She is on her last leg here. Me? Maybe I am not so far behind her. I want to take her somewhere that I can care for her 24/7 and some place where I can be taken care of as well. I want to leave this behind me. I don't want my family to watch me die or suffer. You can visit. I will still visit you and go see Pri, but I must go. It is settled."

"Frannie! What the fuck? Now? When? What? We will take care of you both. Stop this!" I screamed at her.

"Oh, *mi amor*, I love you. I love both of you and the children, grandchildren, and great-grandchildren. Let me ride off into the sunset. Please, this is my wish. Please grant me this."

107

Frannie was adamant. I was in shock as expected. She knew this was the way to present this to us—her bag packed, car ready to go. John moved into her house with their family and took on her part of the farm. It was already taken care of.

"Frannie, *no! No!* I can't let you go. What? Really?"

Luke caressed my arm and gave me a squeeze as a request to accept her proposal. I crawled to her and we hugged a tight hug as we tried to hold in tears.

"When are you leaving?" I asked, not wanting to know.

"Now. I didn't want you to make a fuss, and I can't handle goodbyes. I don't want a big goodbye, Valerie. We leave now. The car is packed."

I gave Frannie a kiss and we held some more.

"Be well, Valerie, we will talk for sure. Luke, take care of this lady and my family."

"I will, Frannie, I will. You are my best friend. I am going to miss you."

We got up and walked with her to the car as John and Clarissa waited with Albina. Marisol came out and ran to the car for a final goodbye on the farm. She got into the car, blew out a kiss, and we watched the dust blow in the wind as they pulled off the property. *I can't believe that she is gone.*

We stood in silence until it became awkward, and I decided to take a walk alone. Marisol came to run after me.

"Mom, are you going to be okay?" she asked in short breaths from running.

"I... ugh... I don't know. Why did you all hide this from me? Why couldn't I just be part of this conversation? Did I miss something? Do y'all not like me enough to want me to know? Do you think I am too old to handle this? I just feel left out and I don't like it," I said, confused.

"No, no. Frannie called John and I for a meeting and told us what she wanted to do. She just didn't want you to get upset and feel like you had to take care of them. She asked us to do this for her. I agree, Mom. You need to relax and enjoy. You do so much for all of us and worry so much. Just please, spend time for yourself with Luke. And help me plan my wedding."

"I will try to… wait, what? Wedding? What?"

She showed me her ring and started jumping in excitement. "Yes! My wedding! I want to have it hear on the farm. Michael asked me last night. Oh, Mom, he is the best! Do you approve?"

"Oh, Marisol, I am so so so excited to hear this! I do approve! So smart of you, Marisol. You are so aware of who you are. I wish I was as strong as you."

"Mom, you are the strongest person that I know. If I didn't watch you, I wouldn't know how to be strong and confident. Michael is so gentle and kind. I am glad that I waited for him."

"I am so happy. When should we plan for the big day?"

"We spoke to the priest and we have a date for the church in June. And then I want to have it here, just like you and Dylan had it. He always told me how wonderful it was. I also want Luke and John to walk me down the aisle. What do you think?"

"I love it! Oh, Marisol, you are so wonderful to include Luke. He really has latched onto all of you, and y'all have embraced him so warmly. He will be so grateful to walk you down the aisle. You are the daughter he always wanted. So now you have three dads! Pretty lucky lady you are."

"Yes, I am. I am lucky to have a relationship with all of them in different ways. Dylan will always be my dad. That will never change."

I kissed her as we walked back to the house, and the pain of Frannie moving away was far back into my memory.

Marisol and I took the ride to see Pri that weekend. She was excited to find out that Marisol was getting married and she could be a bridesmaid. Her health was declining as the disabilities that ailed her had started to take away her short-term memory, and she converted further and further into the little girl she never grew up from. The time staying at this group home was the best thing for her as she had companions and twenty-four hour care. She even had a gentleman that she could have tea parties and walk the farm with. They ate at the same table and he was happy to be called her boyfriend. Dr. Luke had been replaced.

Marisol showed her dresses that she could choose from to wear as the bridesmaid, and she loved all of them. We took her to the store to get measured and find the right shoes to match.

"Marisol, I feel like a princess. Can I wear a crown at the wedding?" Pri asked at the store. Marisol smiled and held her close as they looked in the mirror.

"Oh, a princess like yourself should of course wear a crown. Let's pick one out." They went off to pick one out and I took a minute to look at myself in the mirror, holding a dress up that I found for the wedding.

"Dylan, what do you think, love? Is this my color?"

"Si, *mi amor*. Si. You look beautiful in anything," he answered, and I chuckled. I just thought of Dylan and I walking her down the aisle together. *Oh, Dylan, I miss you so much.*

"I know, *mi amor*, I miss you too. I miss you too. Go and enjoy. Please, please," I heard him say. I closed my eyes to feel him again and touched his watch on my wrist. *He still makes me feel so special.*

Luke became accustomed to his afternoon naps that sometimes grew a little longer than a quick drift off in the big chair in the living room as he read his book under the big lamp. As time moved on after lunch, he retreated to the bedroom and took a two-hour nap, which slowly became a three-hour nap. He would wake up groggy and not sure about the time of day or where he was. At the beginning, he gathered himself together after a few minutes that became a half hour that became the rest of the night. Then the naps became longer. The disorientation soon started in the morning and we needed to put him on a strict schedule. The doctor's said this was the beginning of dementia which scared all of us. It was the beginning of the end.

My handsome boyfriend started to turn into a senior zombie. Each day, his weakness grew, his bold shoulders and arms became gaunt through this time, and soon he was just skin and bones. He must have lost almost sixty-five pounds and fast. His face was withdrawn. When he looked at someone, he looked straight through them. He recognized my voice and perked up as I came close to him. We continued to share the same bed until his night tremors became violent and it was not safe for me to sleep there. We had to sedate him at night, but it still wasn't enough. The decision had to be made to put him into a home. As painful as it was, I had to make some calls and decided what should be done. I called to his ex-wife to see what involvement she wanted in this.

"Hello, how are you?"

"Valerie, what do you want after all these years? Why are you calling me?"

"Well, I just want to let you know that Luke is not well. He is actually very ill. I need to make the decision of putting him into a home, and I just wanted to talk to someone who was somewhat family. Do you want to see him? Do you want to be involved? Do you even want to talk to me? We used to be friends. I just want to give you that respect to know where Luke is at in his health."

"Oh, Valerie, oh, Saint Valerie. Aren't you so special? Oh, I took care of Luke, I saved him, I am fabulous. I think you are an asshole and see through your bullshit. So now you want me to care about Luke? He was a horrible husband to me. So I don't care about what happens to him. Do you think you are special because your husband died, and Luke who always crushed on you now is not well and you want me to take him off your hands? You are a real bitch, Val, I mean, seriously. When Luke and I got a divorce, you never even reached out to me to see if I was okay. I thought we were friends. We spent holidays together. You are a fucking bitch."

"I love Luke. I really do. He is a wonderful companion to me. He was Dylan's best friend. I didn't know him until we started to see each other. It was years after you left him. He has been really hurt in his life. I thought we were friends too. But when Dylan died, where were you? I think you should look in the mirror. I am giving you the respect as a friend and someone that Luke loved, and I believe he still loves you enough to make amends and be a part of his last days. I am doing this for him. I don't want money or to drop him off. I am going to make sure he is well cared for. I just want to do what is right for him.

"So I am grateful that I have been able to spend these last years with him and so grateful that he found me after Dylan died. I am so grateful that my family has embraced him and given him the family he always wanted. So, thank you for letting me know how you really feel, and we will gladly never bother you again. May one day you find Jesus in your heart and one day learn to forgive and understand someone's journey."

With that, I hung up the phone, and as Luke sat in a wheelchair close by, he reached out his hand to me with the little words he had, with the little strength he had. I grabbed his hand back and leaned into him and he held my head close to his, and although he struggled, he gave me a kiss and whispered, "Thank you."

* * * * *

Marisol and Michael were happily married now for years. They hoped for children, and with the help of John and Clarissa, all of them worked the farm and had become one harmonious family. I had to put Luke into a home where I added him into the schedule to spend the day with him after daily mass. Mid-morning was his best time of day. I wheeled him around the grounds and read to him, made sure we caught some sun as the vitamin D was good for him. We held hands, and as he progressed into a deeper state, he was embarrassed and did not look at me. It hurt, but I tried to understand. I still stood by his side.

"I'm not giving up on you, Luke, I love you." I whispered in his ear. He grumbled and situated himself in the chair. His tears he could not hide. I wiped them away and sat on his shoulder. "I'm not giving up, Luke," I said again.

* * * * *

Christopher and Dylan sat on the lawn as Peanut played with her toys in front of them.

"It was the best day of my life to tell my wife in front of God how much I love her again. How happy I was that my whole family was there. John and Clarissa got married, Olivia came back to me. My daughter was away from me most of my life, and she found me on my last day. I can't believe I ended my life because I was so hot-headed and angry. I was so jealous of you. I didn't listen to my heart. That kept me with Valerie. Now we are apart." Dylan was still struggling with his penance and coming to terms with why he ended his life so soon. He wanted to be one with God and live a happy life in heaven. He still had some work to do.

"Dylan, maybe it is not yourself that you need to blame. You were angry, I can understand that. I survived that day and was given a great gift to meet my daughter and spend my last moments on Earth with a woman I chased after my whole life and two of my daughters. You gave me that gift. Maybe you need to look at the situation and the anger you are holding, and maybe you need to look at Valerie. Maybe you need to let her know that you were angry at her and not as much at yourself."

"I never looked at it that way, but you are right. I am angry with her and need to come to peace with that. Thank you, Christopher, that is very helpful." Dylan got up and sat with Peanut to play with her toys. He realized that he was angry with me and didn't know how to approach it. Dylan went to mass and prayed on it and asked Jesus for guidance and help on forgiveness.

Jesus sat and spoke to Dylan, helping him through it. "You will have the chance to talk to her and ask her for forgiveness. Sort it out in your head what you want out of this. Take all the time you need, son." Dylan needed time to process the whole moment.

* * * * *

Marisol and Michael moved into my house and I moved into the guest house. Marisol was a few months pregnant. She was excited to have their child grow up in the same home she grew up in. Michael was very successful, but they wanted to live a humble lifestyle.

"Mom, how are you doing today?" she said to me as now she hosted the morning breakfasts for the family.

"I am good. How are you? I am going to go see Luke today, then go and visit Pri."

"Mom, that is a lot for you. Both in one day? Please take a break. Let's go into town and you can help me look at stuff to decorate the baby's room? We can do lunch, I could use some alone time with you."

"Hmm, I really should go see both."

"You can see them tomorrow. Maybe one, then the other another day? Pri is fine, you saw her on Saturday. Luke doesn't even know you are there. You need a break. It is really bringing you down."

"Luke knows I am there. He perks up when he hears my voice. I just don't want him to be alone."

"Listen, give me today and give Luke tomorrow."

"Okay, I will."

Marisol and I pulled out of the farm in her convertible. Like myself, she never gave up on having a fancy car. She loved the wind in her hair and gave a smile as she drove. It was her personal escape. We got to the furniture store and looked around.

"So what is your color scheme, Marisol? Are you going to find out if it is a boy or a girl?"

"We already have."

"Okay, so when will I find out?"

As I asked, Marisol smirked at me as if to taunt me by her secret. I smiled back at her. "So?"

She walked around the room, expecting me to follow behind her, which I did.

"Mom, what do you think of this crib?" She pointed to a lovely white crib that perfectly suited their bundle of joy.

"I love it, please let me buy this for you guys. I insist."

"That is so nice of you, Mom, it really is. But unfortunately, it won't be enough."

"What? Do you want diamonds on it? This is the one you picked out?"

"It is, but we are going to need two. Can you buy us two?"

"OMG, Marisol. For real? Twins? OMG, this is wonderful new! Marisol, I am so excited for you!" I grabbed her and hugged her in the store. We ordered two cribs. They would be blessed with both a boy and a girl. It could not have been the best news that I needed at that moment. I am eternally grateful. We went to lunch and I sat staring at her in amazement. She was glowing and loving being pregnant.

"Mom, thank you for coming with me today. This is so special."

"Of course, my love. I am so glad that you asked me. I do need to take some time for myself and to spend with you. I love watching you two start your family. John and Clarissa started their family. I am so blessed, I really am. Of course, I always think of Dylan. Oh, how he would have loved to be sitting here listening to this news! Luke would have also loved to hear this news. I can't wait to tell him."

"Mom, what about Christopher? He is also my father. I am sure he would have too. I think about all three of them. I love them all. I have to say, I have been dreaming of Dylan a lot lately. I feel like there is something to it. Like in a good way, that he is with me and trying to tell me something. I don't know, still praying on it to figure it all out."

"Oh, I believe they both are with you, Marisol. Maybe they are together in heaven smiling over us at this moment. I am sure they are both so proud of you. Dylan will let you know when he wants you to know something. He always comes through. Oh, how I love him and miss him so. I can't wait to hold him again."

"That is true. Thanks, Mom. I was agonizing over it. You are right, Dylan always comes through. So does Christopher. Perhaps he is the reason I am having twins. They didn't detect it right away. It was like a crazy miracle. God is good!" She grabbed my hand. It felt different than before. I held onto the moment. That day with her was special. I couldn't place it. Perhaps it was my old age and becoming sentimental. The moment meant the world to me.

"I love you so much, Marisol. I love Michael also. You are both so perfect together. Cherish and enjoy all the moments. They go so quickly."

"Aww, I love you too, Mom. Thank you for my crazy life. I honestly wouldn't have it any other way. I really wouldn't. I can't wait for you to hold these babies!"

We went back to the farm and sat on the porch and waited for Michael to come home. John and Clarissa joined us shortly after. Mary was playing and she came and sat on my lap. I sat next to Marisol and rubbed her stomach. I called out to Dylan and Christopher.

"Hey, boys. Hope that you are together and watching this moment. It would be awesome for you both to be here with us. If it wasn't for both of you, we wouldn't have this. Thank you both for being so loving and forgiving. I don't know how you both put up with me."

*   *   *   *   *

Both Christopher and Dylan sat together and hugged on the news. "See, things are wonderful up here. What a blessing. She is asking for forgiveness, Dylan, I hope you heard that. Please forgive her. You know you want to."

"*Si, si*. I know. I am just having all the old memories. The previous life. The horror. I can forgive this Valerie, but the life before that I never forgave. I believe that is why I took this life. I will forgive that life too. All in its timing, Jesus said to me. I will know when it is the right time."

"Good. Jesus is good."

"Indeed, he is. Indeed, he is."

Christopher and Dylan hugged again. Madeline called over for him to come home for dinner. "Dylan, will you both join us?"

"That is lovely, Madeline, thank you." He gathered Peanut and they all headed over to Madeline's for dinner.

*   *   *   *   *

The third trimester is where we sat, and Marisol, although feeling uncomfortable, wore a smile on her face the whole time. Michael helped her up and out of chairs, walked her down the stairs. He was a perfect husband. I noticed that I was becoming a bit slower in my older age. It took me longer to wake up in the mornings. I gasped for breath going up and down the stairs. My chest didn't feel so right. My right arm tingled. For whatever reason, I decided to ignore the pain and put a smile on my face. I had to be strong and brave for my family.

I went to visit Luke; his dementia was worse. The decision to end the medications and have him drift off into his next life had come. I held him tight. The family came to visit him a few times. I sat at his side, holding his hand, brushing my hands through his hair, giving him kisses. I felt like I prepared for this my whole life—to send him off to his next life. "I love you Luke, I so love you. Do what you have to do," I whispered in his ear. The moment was going to come. I didn't know if I wanted to be here for it or not. I watched him drift. I came in to his lips for a kiss. He moved his lips as much as he could to kiss me back. His skin was hardening. The snores became longer and longer. I kept my touch all over him to console his body.

My phone rang several times within the hour. I felt it was important and needed to answer it.

"Hello?"

"Hello, Mrs. Zavala. This is the director at the farm. I need to alert you that we had a problem with Pri today and she decided to run away. We are looking for her. The police are looking for her. Have you heard or seen her? She has been declining in her health. Her memory, as you know, is not well. We will continue to look for her and keep you posted."

"OMG, do I need to come down? My boyfriend is on his death bed, I really shouldn't leave here. But she is my daughter."

"Mrs. Zavala, there is not a lot you can do. We will stay in touch. Sorry about your boyfriend."

"Okay, I will see if my son can go down there." I hung up the phone. I reached out to John who jumped right in the car and headed to help search for Pri. I had my concentration back to Luke.

The nighttime came, and Luke still held in there. I fell asleep in the reclining chair next to his bed and finally drifted off into a deep sleep. I dreamt of Dylan. We were on the farm. It was the middle of the night and we sat in a stall with the moonlight shining over us. We were naked, draped in a blanket. Neither one of us was asleep.

"Dyl, this feels so real."

"It is a real dream, Valerie, I am here with you. But I must tell you. I have been so angry with you. I was holding it in and blaming myself. I forgive you, Valerie, but my anger at you took my life. I had a hard time dealing with that. I really did. But in heaven, we are taught to forgive and move on. I had a great talk with Christopher who pointed out to me that I needed to forgive you to move on. To help you move on. I learned so much here. I forgive you, Valerie, and I love you. Be strong, Valerie."

He kissed me as he held me close to him. I could not respond. I felt him. It felt so good. I didn't understand what he was saying, but I heard "forgiveness" and "be strong." He did deserve to be angry with me. I hated the lies, the secrets.

"I did it out of love. I was lost, and you found me, Dylan. You loved me and changed me, Dylan. I just want to love you back. Please accept my apology. Jesus, please forgive me. Please forgive me for I have sinned."

Dylan gave me a kiss again on my cheek. "Be strong, my love, forgive. Jesus has heard you. He will forgive you. He always does." Then he was gone, and I was suddenly startled and awake.

"Mrs. Zavala." A nurse was shaking me to wake up. I jumped and caught her eyes.

"Mrs. Zavala, Luke passed away a short time ago. I am so sorry for your loss."

She left the room and gave me some time to say my goodbye to him. He laid there with nothing left in him. I was exhausted with relief for he was no longer in pain.

"Oh, Luke, my love. Find your best friend, Dylan. He will take care of you. Luke, thank you for being Dylan's replacement. I had a wonderful time spending my golden years with you. Find Dylan, he will love you as much as I did. May we meet again one day in heaven. Bye, Luke, you are something so special to me. You won't be forgotten. I love you." I kissed his head, signed the cross on his chest, and with tears down my face, I left the hospital and drove away.

I headed down to Pri's farm as I had to worry about her as well. My pains in my chest were coming through, but I put them aside as I needed to worry about my daughter and then mourn the loss of another man in my life. I arrived at the farm to find John in the lobby. We were still on the hunt for Pri. He was in shock to see me.

"So what is the latest? Any clues as to where she could go?" I asked John.

"They have so many people searching everywhere. I have no idea where she could be. I know at home she had these hiding spots, but I knew where they were. I don't know them here." He was upset and pacing the lobby.

"What about her boyfriend? Does he know where she is?"

He looked at me and rolled his eyes. "Val, I don't mean any disrespect, but none of them can really tell you anything. This is so frustrating."

I also started to pace behind John and it was upsetting to not know where she was and think she was probably in danger. I stopped John as we paced in different directions and grabbed him for a hug. "We will find her. We just need to be strong and pray."

"I am, Momma, I am praying. Jesus, please help my baby sister. I love her so much. Keep her safe and sound. Bring her back to us. Thank you, Jesus."

Pri was found hours later stuck in a tree on the other side of town with Bingo in tow. The fire department had to take hours to get her down as she was there, not remembering or understanding why. She was lost and confused. John and I stood at the bottom of the tree and talked her through it. She was finally rescued and brought into an ambulance.

"Oh, my Pri, I love you, darling. I love you," I said to her as I gave her as many kisses and strong hugs as I could.

"I don't want you to go, Valerie. Please don't go," she said to me.

"Oh, Pri, I am not going anywhere. I will meet you at the hospital." I gave them both a kiss as the doors closed and John stayed with her.

I was relieved. It was a gnarly past few days. I was exhausted by the trauma. The pains in my chest were deep. I ignored them until I couldn't ignore them. I sat in my car, slumped into the steering wheel, holding onto my chest as the beating grew deep; then it stopped, leaving me sweaty and weak. *Just get to the hospital, just get to the hospital, it will be okay. Just hold on.* When the pain stopped, I felt a moment of clarity, and with the top down, I had my window of opportunity to drive myself to the hospital. The wind felt good on my face, and I picked up my pace in speed.

I felt myself a teenager again driving the Pacific highway following Chase, following Taylor. I saw myself walk from Sheila's coffin in a black dress. I chuckled. I saw Richard, now just as old as I was, holding his grandkids, smiling and happy in his life. I saw Ashley at yoga with friends, laughing and enjoying herself, Todd with his family waving at me from afar. I remembered passionate nights with Dylan. The joy of the first cry I heard from Marisol being born. I had a great life, I really had a great life.

"Thank you, Jesus, for my family. Thank you for all that you have given me. Thank you for giving me another chance, I am forever grateful." I smiled as the wind blew in my hair. I felt so free, I felt so alive. The sun was shining. The road became straight. It was a dirt road, and soon I did not notice or know where I was. My heart started to pound again. It was strong. *Hang in there, hang in there, and get to the hospital.*

An animal came out of my side view as I was drifting and my reflexes were not as strong. The car spun and spun. I tried to swerve to avoid the animal in my view. My heart pounded, the car spun. My car slammed into a tree and I was stuck in my seatbelt, the car tilted. Then it was silent. There was no noise. I could not hear myself breathing. I saw a trail of blood form on the side. This was it. Just like that, it was over. I was fading and fading away. I saw the sky, a clear blue. I had a good life. *Jesus, thank you for this wonderful life. Thank you, Jesus. Jesus, I trust in you.*

Then the sky became black, and I felt nothing. It was over. All of it, it was over.

"'For I know the plans I have for you, declares the Lord, plans for welfare and not for evil, to give you a future and a hope'" (Jeremiah 29:11, ESV).

*   *   *   *   *

"Madeline, do I look okay? Is my hair okay? Do you think I should wear pearls? I am so nervous, Madeline, I am so nervous," I asked Madeline as we stood in front of a mirror as she brought me something to wear when she met me at the gates.

"You look fine, dear, you look lovely," Madeline replied.

It was dark and silent. Oh, so silent. I couldn't hear anything. My body was numb to everything. I felt as if I wasn't even there. Then there was a voice.

"Hello, Valerie." It was Peter.

"Hello, wow. Wow. So this is it, huh? Wow." He stood over my body in the car that was turned over. His sweater today was a bright orange and a matching yellow tie. He was so dapper.

"How do you feel, Valerie?" he asked.

"I am not sure. I don't feel anything, just can't believe how fast it was. It was fast. What a life, oh what a life. Wow." He helped me out of the seatbelt and we walked along the dirt road together.

"I am glad for you. I am glad that you had a good life. That is great news. See, I told you that there were people that loved you."

"Yes, you did. You did. I am going to miss the ones I will leave behind. I really will."

"They will miss you too. Don't worry. You will watch over them. They will ask you for guidance You will provide it for them, just as your loved ones watched over you. So now, Valerie, you have some time before you get to the gates. Do as you wish to remember this life. Reflect on it. Say goodbye to your loved ones still here. You can touch things, sleep in your bed, talk to people. Unless they are extremely clairvoyant, they won't hear you or see you. Some may feel you. Just understand that. When you are ready to come to the gates, I will come and escort you."

"Wow, thank you, Peter."

"So what are your questions?"

"Dylan. When do I get to see Dylan?"

"Ah, yes, Dylan. I believe he came to you a few days ago. Listen to his words he said to you. Remember when you first were born and you asked me to go back to your previous life? Well, I told you it wasn't a good one. It wasn't. You turned love into evil and you were not so kind to him. God decided to not send you to hell as he believed that you still have love in your heart, and with his guidance, that strength overcame evil. He, of course, was right. Your strength of love over evil won. Dylan was what you desired, and Jesus gave him to you. You will be together again, you will. Finish your business here. He is anxiously waiting for you. See you, Valerie."

Then as we stopped, Peter was gone. I was alone in this dirt road, unaware of where it was. I walked straight, learning the new ghost form that I was. Love overcame evil, love gave me my miracle. Love gave me Dylan, a family, fortune. Love gave me a relationship with God and a ticket to heaven. Love gave me forgiveness. Love overcame evil.

I walked until I was able to get myself to the farm where Pri was. She was back from the hospital and John was with her as she slept in her bed, holding Bingo. I came in to give her a kiss and sit by the side of the bed. She opened her eyes and smiled. "Hi, Valerie," she whispered and closed her eyes again. John moved to look at her. She went right back to sleep. I laid next to her and caressed her hair. She snuggled into Bingo and smiled in her sleep. She was my angel on Earth.

John was pouting and holding his bottom lip. He was so much like Dylan. I came to hug him from behind. He couldn't feel me. He was upset and lost. I whispered in his ear, "John, I love you. Don't be upset, enjoy life. Enjoy your family. You are the man of this family, Mr. Zavala. Make us all proud."

He sighed as if he heard me and came to peace with himself. He sat down with Pri and rubbed her back, and she snored away with a smile on her face. He left for the evening and drove home to Clarissa. I sat in the car with him as I didn't want him to be alone. John spoke to himself as he drove.

"Wow, my parents are all gone. I am the head of the family now. This is such a feeling. This farm has seen some history for sure. Oh, Valerie, please find Dylan. Oh, I love you both so much." He shed tears that he wanted to get out of the way before he came home to Clarissa, before he had to tell Marisol who was so very pregnant. He had to be strong for all of them. So he wept. "Oh, Valerie, I wish I was as strong as you were. I already miss you so much." He continued his tears.

I crawled to him and held as tight as I could. I gave him kisses, and knowing he couldn't hear me, I rode with him and spoke to him. "Oh, John, you are a strong man. You have a heart of gold. I will always be with you, my love. You are the son I always wanted. Thank you for being in my life, following your dreams, and making us so happy."

He stopped his tears and pulled into the farm. He collected himself and gathered his thoughts.

*   *   *   *   *

Marisol was asleep when Dylan came to visit her. "I am so excited for these babies to be born young lady."

She was sleeping, but felt the dream was so real. It was. "Dylan, this feels so real."

"It is my love. It is. I know you asked why I keep coming to you. It's time. Valerie is gone. Be strong, girl. Be strong for your brother and sisters. Be strong for your family. We love you and will watch over you. She will visit you when she is ready, I know she will. I love you, Marisol." He gave her a kiss and she felt it.

She awoke and felt that I was gone. She knew it. She walked outside just as John pulled in. She ran to the car and hugged him.

"Marisol, oh, I needed that hug. I need to talk to you." John hugged her as tight as he could. He led her to the patio.

"I know. Valerie is gone. I just had a dream."

"Wait, you know from a dream? How?"

"Dylan has been coming to visit me. I thought it is because I am about to give birth. But he kept talking to me and I didn't understand what he was saying. He just came to me and told me she was gone. When I woke up, I felt it. John, I felt it. So is she gone?"

There was a pause as they held hands. Clarissa came out with a jacket for both.

"Yes, Valerie died. She had a heart attack after we found Pri. She was driving, and the car hit a tree. Marisol, the scene was so horrible. Her face was so empty. She is in a better place, Marisol. She will be with Dylan. I just know it."

Clarissa went behind Marisol and hugged her as she too was mourning my loss. "Now, Marisol, let's get you to rest. Valerie does not want you to strain yourself over this. She would ask you to take care of those babies and pay her no mind."

Marisol chuckled at Clarissa's comment as it was true. I would do as Frannie would and smack some asses and demand no tears. They went back into my old home and Marisol went into bed. Michael came home from work and crawled in with her, his hand caressing her stomach. She fell asleep next to him.

* * * * *

Dylan watched from his window, anxious for my arrival. Madeline came from across the street and waved to him as she went to the front door and entered the house.

"Hello, Dylan!" she shouted to him.

He went downstairs to greet her.

"How are you today? Are you okay?"

"Yes, Madeline. I am good. Maybe over-anxious. I just can't wait for her to be here. I miss her so much."

"I know, Dylan, I know. Relax. She will be here. Have you forgiven her?"

"I did, I did. Now I just want to hold her again. I am so excited to see her. I missed her so much, y'all have no idea."

"I can't wait. It will be wonderful. Rejoice! She will be here soon. I just wanted to come and give you a hug. I am going to pick her up at the gates. Leaving soon."

"Thank you, Madeline. Thank you."

She went back to her home and left Dylan alone in his thoughts.

*   *   *   *   *

I went about the houses that night and kissed them all good-night as they slept. I told them how much I missed them and would watch over them. I walked outside to tour the farm in the moonlight. It was so different from this side of the fence. I felt weightless. It was weird to not be present. It was also peaceful. I walked to the rose patch and past the benches in the woods. Then there was Luke waiting for me.

"Hello, Valerie," he said.

126

"Luke! OMG! I didn't know I would ever see you again!" I ran to him and gave him a hug. It was real.

"Yes, Valerie, I am here. I feel good. I am so happy to see you."

"Luke, wow, this is so crazy."

"It is as I have a few moments ahead of you. I agree, it is crazy. Oh, Valerie, it is awesome to feel good again, to talk to you again. I was so broken. The last years were hard to be so sick. But Valerie, you made me feel as good as I could be. It really helped me through, having you and the kids. I love those kids as if they were my own. I am so grateful."

"Luke, I feel like when you found me in the stall that day, I never remembered that you existed. You came into my life at that time for a reason. You are the one that saved me. I have to believe that Dylan, with God's help, brought us together."

"Oh, Valerie, I know that is true. Dylan came to me in a dream a few weeks before that day and he told me to go and help you out. That you were sad and lonely. So I did. I didn't expect to fall in love with you, I really didn't. I never believed I could fall in love again, and I didn't."

"Wait, I am confused? You said you loved me, but you weren't in love with me?"

"Yes, I fell in love with you. I did. I had never had been in love before. You gave that to me. I love the family you gave me. I am so blessed. I know you and Dylan are excited to see each other again. I respect that. I am at peace and will spend my time in heaven with love in my heart until I am ready to go back again. I am so happy that you will be back with Dylan again. He really misses you."

"Luke, that is so sweet. I loved you too. I admired the friendship you and Dylan had. I really enjoyed every moment being with you. You were a nice person to be around. I cherished our moments. You were so kind and caring to me. I felt the love. You filled the void I was missing from Dylan."

"You always missed him."

"I did, I really did."

"So, Valerie, where else do you wish to go from here? What do you want to visit?"

127

"I don't know. I didn't spend much time other than at the farm. Maybe go home to California, go home to NYC, then end in Larchmont where it all began. I just don't want to leave them. I guess I don't have a choice."

"You will always be in their heart. Go and see those places and visit. Do you want me to come with you?"

"I'd love that. I love spending time with you. Where do you want to go, Luke?"

"I already went to all the places I wanted to visit. I am content. I just want to be with you until it is time for me to go to the gates. I want to hold you as long as I can."

So off we went. We walked through the woods and walked onto the beach where Tom's house was. "So, Luke, this is where I spent my teenage years. On this beach. There was Tom's house. It was peaceful here." We walked into the house and walked around. There was a new family here since Tom had passed years ago. They didn't change much. I sat with Luke at the dining room table as the family that occupied that space was having dinner. We held hands and I decided to take him to my old bedroom. It was now a young teenage boy's room. We snuggled on the bed and I told him stories of my vision board that appeared as I spoke. He could see Cal and Madeline running on the beach and the visions I built of Christopher. It was a different life.

We traveled to Larchmont. We entered my childhood home. The feelings were different. The house had love in it. The kitchen island was white instead of the dark we grew up with. It was bright and warming, not gloomy which we grew up with. I went up to my bedroom and sat at the front of the door and felt the memories of when Sheila died, and I sat with my brother and sister to send her off into the light. I hoped that she found the light.

My next stop was the attic. I held Luke's hand into the attic and we laid on the floor together. It was refurbished since the fire. That was the last time I was up here. Luke and I laid on our backs and smiled at each other. I felt at home.

"I feel like a kid again," I said to Luke. He held my hand and looked into my eyes.

"You are home. I am so glad I met you, Valerie, so glad. You gave me life." The flashes started, his grip was becoming loose.

"Thanks for the ride, kid, I will be so blessed to ever see you again."

The flashes grew bigger, his grip loosened. Peter appeared and took his hand, and then they were gone.

"I won't forget you, Luke. I won't forget you."

He was gone and then there was silence; a loud silence. I stayed on the floor and couldn't feel anything. I laid there alone. My mind started to drift. I remembered the farm. The musk of the morning. I remember the smell of hay. I remember the slamming of the front door. Meals at the island. My children surrounding me with love. There was always love. There was always love when I had Dylan. There was always love once I figured out that I needed to love myself.

"Thank you, Jesus, for this life you gave me. Thank you for your favor. I am so blessed. I am ready for you. I am ready." It was silent, then my surrounding became dismal, my vision became blurry. I closed my eyes. I saw clouds. I felt my body moving. It was almost as if I was on a bobsled. It was fast. I stayed calm. Then it stopped.

I opened my eyes. I was back in the white room with no definition, no doors. No sign of anyone. I waited patiently, and before long, Peter appeared, this time in a red sweater and blue tie.

"Hello, Miss. How are you today? Are you ready?"

"I am good. I am ready."

"A much different reaction from when we last sat here. Good, good to hear. Now I have processed your paperwork and you are ready to go. Enjoy your time here. Enjoy meeting Jesus and ask him anything and everything. He is always here for you. Stay if you like. The only rules are:

- Learn to forgive.
- Love as much as possible.
- Let go of your anger.
- Reflect on what you were on Earth and what lessons you learned to be a better person in your next life.
- Enjoy your time here.
- Feel the love that Jesus gives you."

"I think I can do that."

"Perfect, then it is settled. Madeline is waiting for you. She is right on the other side."

With that, he pushed through the wall and a new world came before it. It was bright and beautiful like a huge garden in France. The flowers were spectacular! The greens were vibrant. The gate was in gold and massive. The other side was a very excited Madeline waving and as anxious as I was to finally meet. I came through the other side and we ran to each other to hug. Peter watched from the other side and waved goodbye as I was in his sight.

"Madeline! OMG! Madeline, you are real, it is you. You are everything to a tee that I imagined. I can't believe this!"

She smiled and smiled. "Oh, my dearest Valerie, your thoughts were always so vivid because I was so real in your mind. I was there. We are so in tune with each other. I never stopped giving up on you, Valerie. It could have gone down a bad path. But you are a strong woman. What you have become, I am so proud."

We hugged again. Her smell was like a bouquet of flowers. She wore the dress I imagined her in. She was forever my idol. *She is now with me. I am so blessed.*

*   *   *   *   *

John called the family over to the rose patch. He had some champagne and glasses which he opened and handed out to everyone. They stood in a circle around the patch, and John held up his glass for a toast.

"This morning we buried two more people that we loved. They join the others that live here from our family. Peanut's spirit, of which this rose patch was created for, Dylan, Frannie, Albina, Tom, and Brenda. Now we lift our glasses to two more, Valerie and Luke. Luke, you were always a part of our family since I was young. You and Dylan were best friends. I am so grateful that you and Valerie found each other when she really needed someone. You became a big part of the family. We love you.

"Valerie, my mother. The woman who raised me. Who raised us. Who took us into her arms when our father died. When our mother could not care for us. You loved us without even knowing us. Gave us all a future. I am so proud to have known you. I had a career I would not have dreamed of if it wasn't for her support and encouragement. I would not have had the courage to ask Clarissa out on a date if you didn't push me. Oh, Valerie, Momma. I love you so. We all love you and miss you. Please go and find Dylan. May we all meet again one day in heaven."

He held up his glass as they all cheered each other. They spent the rest of the night on the porch with tequila, telling stories, and laughing. It was just the send-off I wanted.

*   *   *   *   *

Madeline brought my red dress that Dylan bought me in Disney. She brought my perfect pink pumps that I wore when I was young and cute, when I started dating Dylan.

"No, no pearls, wear this instead," she said and handed me my love necklace. She fixed my hair the way Dylan always complimented that he liked it—all pushed over to one shoulder, straight, and long. We walked toward the house. I was anxious. I was so nervous to see him. I could not wait to see him.

"Don't worry, he is just as nervous. He really is."

As we walked, I had so many questions for Madeline. "So did you find Cal? Will he be here too?" Oh, Cal, yes. I found him, of course. He left us not that long ago. He went to be with a nice family. I think you will approve," she said.

"What does that mean? He left? What family?"

"Oh, Valerie, you will learn so much up here. We all travel in circles. Didn't anyone on Earth remind you of someone and you maybe couldn't place it?"

"Hmm, I guess. I have to think about it. Can you give me a hint?"

"I could, but think of your grandchildren. Think of who they remind you of."

"Mary is my first grandchild, and then the other two haven't been born yet. Wait, Mary?"

"Yes, my dear. Mary is Cal."

"What?"

"Oh, yes, my dear, yes. So much happens up here. Soak it all in. It is a fascinating place."

We got closer to the house, and Madeline stopped me on the corner before it was in sight. She held me by my shoulders. "I am so glad that you are here, Valerie. God is good, he brought you and Dylan back together again. It is a wonderful gift. Cherish it."

"I will, Madeline, I will."

We approached the house, and Dylan sat on the lawn chair, 'olding his bottom lip, combing his hand through his hair. He was nervous awaiting my arrival. He came into sight and I stopped moment. I saw him stand up in slow motion. He was almost in cloudy vision. He was the young Dylan I met so many years ago at a Yankee game. He was in a suit, holding roses. He saw me and smiled. I knew that everything was going to be okay.

I ran to him and he ran to me. We caught in each other's arms and he twirled me around, held me in the air, and slowly brought me down to him. It was the reminder of the first time I came to Houston. The embrace was so warm. I longed for him forever. My blessing was with me. My angel was in my arms.

"Oh, Dylan, it was always you."

*   *   *   *   *

"Daddy, Daddy!" Marisol called in her sleep. Michael was in a stage four state of REM; he didn't hear her. "Daddy, oh, Daddy, I need you!" She was becoming restless as the twins came closer to being born. She was uncomfortable, so nervous to be a mom for the first time. She had her husband, she had her brothers and sisters. She didn't have her parents. She was feeling the effects of us being gone. "Daddy..." she said in a long drawn-out cry for him.

$$* \quad * \quad * \quad * \quad *$$

Dylan and Christopher watched over her and felt her pain. "I think you should go. She is talking to you, Dylan," Christopher said to him.

"I thank you, and I believe she is too. I love her with all my heart," Dylan replied as he held his bottom lip.

"I know you do. I do too. You were very important to her. Now go."

Dylan took a deep breath and brought himself into her bedroom. He knelt next to the bed and held her forehead. "I am here princess, *mi amor*, I am here. It is Daddy."

"Daddy, I miss you. I am so scared. Where is Mommy? Is she with you? I need both of you. I can't do this without you both." Marisol cried with her eyes closed and in a state of REM.

"I know, *mi amor*, it is hard. You are strong like your mother. We will be there with you. Don't be scared. Let Michael take care of you. Mommy is with me in heaven. So are Christopher and Peanut. We are all here watching over all of you. I love you so much, Marisol, we all do." He rubbed her arm and gave her kisses to her head.

She smiled and was able to control her sobbing. At that time, Michael turned over as he started to hear her. He lifted himself up as he could feel someone else in the room and saw Dylan caring for Marisol. He froze in astonishment. Dylan looked up at him and smiled.

"I will, Daddy, I love you." Dylan stayed for a few more moments and then went back to heaven.

She was at peace and Michael, not fully awake, went back into his pillow and pulled Marisol a bit closer. They went into a deep sleep until the morning.

The alarm went off and both were not prepared as they slept so soundly. She opened her eyes and twisted about to wake themselves up. Michael shut off the alarm then went back to hold his head into Marisol's.

"I think I saw your dad last night," he said to her.

She was still processing being awake. "Oh, my gosh, wait! Now that you are saying that, I had a dream about him. I felt him. Whenever he comes to me in a dream, it feels so real. I can believe it was him standing over me."

"I just thought of it as I was waking up. That is crazy. Well, good to know that you have loved ones around you." He got up and went into the shower.

Marisol needed extra time to get herself up and out as her belly was controlling the weight of her small frame. She went quietly out to the rose patch and knelt to say a prayer.

*   *   *   *   *

As Dylan embraced me in that moment, he took the chance to stop me and point to the rose patch where Marisol was kneeling. I didn't know we had the ability to see them. This feeling was so unreal.

"I paid a visit to Marisol right before you got here. She was so upset. I went to console her. She is going to be okay. Jesus will come soon and show you it will be okay. The babies will be familiar. She will always have us watching over her."

I didn't know what that all meant just yet. I was soaking it all in. I was so lucky to have Dylan again. I couldn't stop touching his face with my cheek, soaking in his scent, his touch on my arm, his kiss on my lips. We walked, slowly admiring each other, and held hands to his house.

Madeline walked behind us, also enjoying the first encounter we all had. She remembered her own encounters for the first time seeing everyone. She remembers her first time seeing Christopher and the love they shared in a previous life.

As we walked to the house, Dylan stopped at the front porch. "I have someone very excited to meet you." I was nervous as I could not think of who I was about to meet. We entered the house and there was a small girl playing with toys on the couch. She was about four years old, crazy curls, and dressed in the cute dress I had picked out for her once I knew I was having a baby. It was Peanut. I held my hand to my mouth as she was the image I had of her in my head. The pain in my stomach, imagining her in a red bag in the trash. She was now real in this world I lived in. She looked up and smiled.

"Momma!" she said and ran to give me a hug. The love in her heart was visible and the reunion I never thought I would have was happening. *This is truly heaven.*

"OMG, Peanut, I love you so much!" I gave her another hug that she gladly accepted. We sat on the couch together as a family and played with her toys. It was peaceful. It was the dream I had for us when I came to Texas. We were home.

*   *   *   *   *

Marisol was uncomfortable in her last days of being pregnant. She struggled with emotions and what it would be like to give birth to twins, a boy and a girl. She wandered around the farm and into John and Clarissa's house. They all held an open-door policy. Clarissa was dropping off Mary at school, and Marisol went up into the attic to see if she could find her old baby blanket. She searched around and found her box of baby items. There was the blanket Pri and Frannie made for her. She hugged it and let her finger line out the feather on the back.

"Oh, Mom, it reminds me so much of you." She started to cry. Marisol laid on the floor and cried, but as she was so big, she was not able to get up. She laid on the floor and listened to the sounds of the house.

"Let's all be with her," Dylan said, and we found ourselves surrounding the floor of the attic sitting with Marisol.

Peanut played with Lucky and curled into Marisol to hug her. "Look into that bag over there, those are my things from Momma. I want you to have them for the babies," Peanut said in her ear.

Marisol moved her head to look over. She tried to roll over and groaned out loud in frustration just as Clarissa came in with a bang from the front door slamming behind her.

"Hello?" Clarissa screamed out. "Marisol?" she asked.

"Clarissa! I am in the attic. Can you help me?"

Clarissa went running to her. "Marisol, what are you doing up here?" She was laughing as Marisol's position in the floor was kind of funny. She was also draped in her baby blanket.

"Stop laughing at me and help me up!"

Clarissa did.

"Can you help me get that box up there?"

"Sure, what is that? What does it say on it? Peanut?" It was written on the side, very small as it was still our secret.

"Yes, please," Marisol said and found somewhere to sit near the window.

"What is Peanut? Is this still your parents stuff? We never really went through it when we moved in," Clarissa said as she struggled to get the dusty box down.

"It is my sister's name. She died before she was born," Marisol said very straightforward.

Clarissa looked back as she did not know there was another Zavala. "What?" she said as the box dropped down to the floor. She pushed it over to Marisol.

"Yes, my parents had a baby and lost it when they went to Mexico. I don't know the whole story, but no one knows but me that they were expecting."

"Wow," Clarissa said.

"Yeah, wow. I have no idea what is in this box, but someone just whispered in my ear that I should open it. I must believe it is a message from all of them."

Dylan, Peanut, and I held close to each other and sat as close to her as we could. Marisol opened the box and took a deep breath as she saw the gingham sheets in both blue and pink. There were some dresses and a few onesies, all for newborns.

"OMG, this is crazy. Perfect timing. Marisol, this is so from your parents!"

"No, it's from Peanut," Marisol said.

Clarissa found an envelope labeled Dylan. It was bulky as it had something in it. She handed it to Marisol. Marisol took another breath and opened the envelope. It was the pregnancy stick and the sonogram of Peanut only a few months old. Then there was a note:

> Dylan, my love,
>   I am so grateful that you came into my life.
> I am so grateful that you asked me to be here. I
> am so grateful that we will be growing our family

together. I love you, Dylan. I am so excited to tell you that you are going to be a dad. I wouldn't want our life to be any other way. I can't wait to be your wife and share this with all of you.

PS: To Peanut Zavala, we can't wait for you to get here. There will be nothing but love here for you. XOXOXO

Love,
Valerie

Dylan moved into me with tears. He never knew the box existed as this was the first time we all saw this. Marisol and Clarissa cried, and Peanut smiled.

"Mom, that is so lovely. Thank you for being my mom. I want to give all this love to Marisol and her babies. They are ready for her. They are coming soon. They are ready," Peanut said to us. We went back to our living room, and Dylan decided to cook dinner for us. Peanut and I cuddled on the couch and admired the smells of chicken cutlets and coleslaw being made.

Clarissa helped Marisol back to her house. They were both amazed to tell their husbands of what they just found. It was a moment to cherish.

"They are coming soon, I feel it. I can feel our family surrounding us. That was a gift, Marisol. Let's go and pray around the rose path," John said.

They all got up and moved to the rose path, held hands, and thanked God and us for the gifts they found and the gifts of two babies about to enter their family.

Dylan called us for dinner and we said a prayer back to them as we sat to eat. As the two worlds we lived in today, we were all together. *It is amazing to be here in heaven. It is amazing to love your family from above.*

"Marisol, I love you so much," I said to her, and she smiled as I knew she heard me.

*   *   *   *   *

The next day, Madeline came by after mass.

"Hello!" she sang and walked into the kitchen. I was making breakfast. Dylan stood with his coffee next to the stove so we could admire each other. Madeline stood in the doorway of the kitchen in her perfect uniform and heels, smiling as she loved to see Dylan smile—to have us all as a family. She held a bunt cake.

"Oh, Valerie, I love that you are making Dylan's favorite breakfast. Here is a bunt cake to top it off. Will you come over for dinner tonight?" Madeline asked.

Dylan looked at her and then me as he sipped his coffee.

"Absolutely, thank you for the invite. Please stay for breakfast, Madeline." I asked.

"Oh, no, no. We already ate. I can't wait for you to meet my family, Valerie. I am sure you will be so happy," she said.

I took no notice or understanding to what she was saying. "I can't wait. We can't wait," I said as I kissed Dylan and then Peanut, then turned back to her eggs. They smiled as they knew what I did not.

* * * * *

The pains were getting worse. Marisol cried on the couch and started to ask for things to grasp and hold the pain. Michael took her to the couch to sit and figure out her level of pain.

"Hey love, how are we doing? Where is the pain?" he asked.

Marisol screamed at the top of her lungs and grabbed her abdomen. "They are coming now! I don't think we have time to go to the hospital. It is now!"

"Okay, love, I am calling 911!"

The ambulance came after several loud screams.

*   *   *   *   *

That evening, we went over to Madeline's for dinner, and Christopher answered the door. I did not recognize him. "Hello," he greeted us. Of course, Dylan and Peanut were very familiar with this environment and smiled as I had put them out of my mind, and now they were not recognizable to me.

"Hello, I am Valerie," I said and went to shake Christopher's hand.

He smiled and looked at me, hoping that I recognized him. Dylan put his hand on Christopher's shoulder and asked to start the evening off with some tequila as we used to drink on the deck in the late afternoons. They walked away to the back deck talking, and Peanut went to go play beside them.

"Valerie, come and meet my daughter and granddaughter." She escorted me into the kitchen as they were making dinner. I stopped placing Madeline with an association to my family. In my head, she was a fabulous movie star that I admired from afar. She became a friend in my fantasy. She was real in my dreams and now, in heaven, she was my neighbor.

"Valerie, this is my daughter, Sheila, and my granddaughter, Ashley." She let it be and I shook their hands. I had put them so far out of my mind I did not recognize them. Sheila decided to speak up.

"Valerie, I have missed you so much. I am so happy to be here with you." She came in for a hug that was long and confusing. I didn't recognize her. Ashley came behind her and gave me a hug.

"I missed you, little lady! Glad that you are here. Thank you for being here with us," Ashley said.

I accepted the hugs but was confused about who they were. I looked at Madeline as I blushed and excused myself as the only safe-haven I ridiculously felt here in heaven was with Dylan. I went out to him and picked up Peanut for security and ran to stand directly in front of Dylan.

He stood up and assured me everything was okay and took Peanut out of my arms so we could walk away for a few minutes.

"*Mi amor*, what is wrong? Nothing is bad here in heaven. Nothing. Are you okay?" He held me close as I wanted to cry, but it wasn't coming out. There were no tears here. He consoled me until I realized my anxiety was just a human reaction. It wasn't real. I kept breathing until I relaxed. I was very confused as to who these people were and why they knew me, and I didn't know them.

"*Mi amor*, just relax. You are in good hands here. Think about who they are to you. Look at their faces. It will all come to you. You will understand everything. You will."

"Dylan, can you just tell me? I am nervous."

He held me tighter. "I can, but you need to see it for yourself. It is all okay. You are okay. Jesus is here, you will be meeting him soon. He will let you know that it is all okay. But you must meet these ladies and understand who they are. It will make the process faster and you will be relaxed. It will be just fine, my love. I won't leave your side."

With that, Madeline came over to announce that dinner was ready and we should sit at the table. Dylan held my hand as we went to sit down, and I was directly across from Sheila. We held hands to say grace and started our meal together.

"Valerie, I know this is hard for you. I understand how it feels. I just want to tell you that I always loved you. I was so jealous of you because you were so strong and had your father Tom's attention when I couldn't. I always thought he was the love of my life. I was not the person I wanted to be. I am now. I hope that you will see that I am now. Please forgive me for all the horrible things I have done to you. I want you to know that I loved watching you take care of your family and how they are so loving and caring. Your heart was pure, and it showed. All the children are beautiful, especially Peanut right here. I admire you. I admire your love for Dylan, how you searched and kept him in your heart, even when you thought he was someone else. You made sure that you found him, and you did. I will keep that with me when I go into my next life and keep that promise to God in my heart that I did not have on Earth. I pray and will ask you for forgiveness so when I move on, there will be no hurt in my heart."

I looked up and around the table as I chewed my food. I was processing her words and still confused by them. I was ashamed for not knowing. I took a minute to look at my hand. I had the cloth ring on that Dylan gave me in Mexico from the girls that was refurbished for our second renewal. I touched my shirt and moved to my neck to touch my pearls. I held the pearls as if they gave me an answer.

"Thank you for restringing my pearls and keeping them with you. They looked better on you anyway," Sheila said.

"Sheila? Mom? No, sorry, Sheila, it is Sheila." I started out soft, but the memory was strong. The reminder, *"Don't call me Mom!"*

Sheila let out a sigh and tried to stand up from the table to move closer to me.

I held onto Dylan. "It is okay, Valerie. It is a lot at once. It is okay," he whispered into my ear.

Sheila sat back down and held her hand to her forehead on the table.

"I was a horrible person. No one should ever tell their daughter that, to never call her mom. I am so horrible. Forgive me, Valerie. I have nothing but love for you and did my best up here to send love to you and your family. Valerie, I want to make up for lost time and be the mother I never was to you in this short time that I am up here. I want to go back to Earth and teach all that I have learned from your love to others, to spread the joy you had. Forgive me, Valerie."

Dylan kept his face close to mine and held my hand, giving it a squeeze. His touch was so comforting. He whispered in my ear, "When I came here, I found Lydia and Miguel. They asked me to forgive them and move on. I looked at Sheila and Ashley and turned to you and asked you if you could forgive them. You said yes with no hesitation." He left it at that. I turned into his face and gave him a kiss and backed away from him to look at Sheila.

"I forgive you, Sheila, I forgive you. Please, take the love and use it to teach others on Earth how to be kind and loving. It gave me a new life that I didn't think I deserved. I forgive you, and I want to grow here in heaven so I will forgive." We got up and hugged across the table. Everyone cheered and drank in merriment.

Ashley came up beside me for a hug. "Valerie, I was not the best to you. I thank you for giving me Chase as he was the best thing that happened to me. I thank you for the lovely speech at my funeral, for even coming to my funeral. I hope that you can forgive me too."

I hugged her back. "I forgive you, Ashley, I forgive you."

"Good, thank you. That is the last piece I needed before I moved on. I feel it coming, it is close. Do you, Sheila?"

"I do, the voices are coming closer. Jesus will be here soon. I know it," Sheila said.

We finished our dinner and laughed. We sat outside around the fire and held each other close. Dylan held Peanut on his chest as she played with his cross, and I held my hand on her back as she started to drift into sleep. I looked at Christopher as I hadn't yet processed who he was. It was a lot for one day.

The next day, we came home from mass, and Madeline screamed for us to come to the front yard. "It is time!" she screamed.

We gathered around in a circle, and Ashley and Sheila stood in the center as Jesus arrived. He asked that we all prayed and if there were any ill feelings, we should clear them now before these ladies were sent back to Earth. I felt good and free from the hatred from them and said a beautiful goodbye that I would keep with me. They went back down to Earth as a boy and a girl. We sat with Jesus as he gave us all as much time as we needed with him.

"Valerie, you have found love in your heart, and I am proud of you to forgive your mother and sister. It will make for a loving future for them on Earth."

"Thank you, Jesus, I feel good about it. I love it up here. I am so grateful to have my family with me. Thank you for having me here. I understand my life before was not good, and you saved me. I hurt people and should have been sent to hell, but you saw good in my heart and saved me. I thank you for believing in me."

Jesus replied, "You were not a good person and killed your own. I did see good in you and sent you back right away as your penance. You kept me in your heart, I gave you a new chance at life. You made me proud when you went back to Mexico and forgave Pedro. That was a big piece of love in your heart. You were the same as him in a previous life, and you did not seek forgiveness."

I sat on the couch with Dylan and Peanut as we watched Marisol give birth to a twin boy and girl in the living room of our home. It was our next evolution.

Dylan and I sat on the couch after Peanut went to bed, and we started to have some of the conversations that we left behind in the previous life.

"I saw you when you went down to Mexico for Olivia's wedding," Dylan said. He held me tight as we had a fire lit and admired the glow and warmth. Everything up here was so beautiful, and you soaked up each piece. "You did forgive him, Valerie. That was a big piece of your development. We have so much to talk about and discuss."

"We do, my love. I know we do. I am so overwhelmed with everything. But it is all good. I did forgive Pedro, I felt that I had to for the family. But now, seeing Peanut, it is hard to know what she could have been. But she has love in her heart. She does."

"I don't know if she forgave him. I don't know that I did either, Valerie. He didn't make it to heaven."

With Dylan's words, I saw Pedro in hell where it was dark and gloomy. I didn't understand how Lydia made it to heaven and he did not; how Jesus saved me and not him. "Oh, Jesus, help me understand. Dylan, what can we do?"

He held me closer as we felt the fire on us. We sat in silence for the rest of the evening. Not everyone could forgive so quickly.

*   *   *   *   *

Olivia came to stay with Marisol when she was home from the hospital to help navigate two babies at once. Olivia became a nurse and stopped after she had children of her own. Her husband was very successful and was able to provide for their family very generously. He encouraged Olivia to spend as much time with the family as possible while he was on the road between the businesses. She came along with her kids as they were off from school.

Olivia loved to spend time with babies as she always felt they were reincarnated and not used to their new lives yet. I could agree. When I was born as Valerie, I remembered my past life. I knew I belonged to something else. I wanted it back at that time. I had no idea that I was a bad person. Now I questioned everything.

Olivia held Marisol's son, James, and spoke to him asking questions. She may not find the answers too for some time.

"James, my love, who are you? Where did you come from? Oh, your grandparents must be so proud of you. I wish they were here to meet you." It was just before dawn and the sky was clear. She watched out the window to enjoy the farm at this time. James was content in her arms and Marisol held her daughter, Britney, in her arms at the other side of the house, just within earshot to hear Olivia and smile. They walked back and forth to keep the babies at peace. Marisol looked out the window and saw a feather fly toward her.

"OMG!" she yelled and ran with Britney out the door to catch it. Olivia was concerned and walked toward her. Marisol came back into the house with a tear and sat down as Britney did not feel affected by her cry.

"Are you okay? What happened?" Olivia said. She held her free hand on the table and looked at this with astonishment.

"Olivia, I don't know how much you know of my mother. When Dylan died, you came back into our lives. I am grateful. My mom always told us to pay attention to the signs and symbols that God gives us. She always caught feathers, and as she held them, she said who spoke to her from above. I was listening to you and I felt a presence, so I looked up, and outside I saw this feather flying toward me. I know it was her. She is here, and it feels so wonderful!" Marisol broke down.

Olivia took the babies back into their crib for their early morning sleep. When they were safe, she went over to Marisol and held her for as long as she needed. "Marisol, that is wonderful. I feel them here with us too. I keep telling you, those babies are from our cycles of life. I have something I want to tell you, Marisol. I never told anyone before." Olivia was serious and felt a bond at that moment with Marisol. She needed to talk to someone and let go of the pain she held as this was a time she needed to, for these babies.

"Marisol, I always felt that I remembered stuff from a previous life. So not that long ago, I went to see a spiritual woman who helped me go through past lives and find out who I was. I found out that I was tortured and beaten by a boyfriend who wasn't even a boyfriend. I had in my head that it was. I was his slave and he continued to rape me and hurt me. There were others too. The stories she told me gave me chills down my spine. It helped me to know as I always felt betrayed by life and family. There was something about Valerie that drew me to her, and then I felt this hatred, anger. I was so young and loved Dylan so dearly. My mother put bad thoughts in my head. She never told me that Dylan was my real father. Pedro did when she died.

"I had a dream before my mother found out that she was sick, and it was back to my previous life being tortured. I didn't realize it was from a previous life. When I spoke to this spiritual woman, she hypnotized me to go back to that dream. It was horrible, and I felt the pain. I was able to look him in the eye, and when I did, I saw his eyes… and it was Valerie. I didn't know why I was so mad at her, but I stayed in Mexico by choice as I felt a hatred towards her and didn't know why. When I did that hypnosis, I understood.

"This spiritual woman helped me work through the feelings and emotions. She also believes from looking at a picture that it was Valerie also. She helped me to forgive Valerie, and through time, I forgot about it and was able to forgive. So I came to the wedding as Valerie never gave up on finding me. That night, when Dylan died, I remembered it again and the feelings were horrible. I blamed her for Dylan's death. But I went to work with that spiritual advisor that told me to give her love to drive away the hatred from the past lives. It helped break the ugly cycles, and it will bring us all closer to Jesus. It really has brought me closer to him. Now I know this whole story sounds crazy, and I don't want it to change how you think of Valerie. I don't blame her for Dylan's death. I do believe that they are together watching over us. I really do. I believe whoever she was in a previous life was a horrible person. I think she really believed in God and it helped her in this life. Y'all had a good life here, I am blessed that I came back to be a part of the family and make up for lost time.

"I know that she did not have a good relationship with her mother and sister. I have to say, I think these babies are them. I don't know why. I just do. So I ask them these questions, and then the feather came. There is no accident there."

Olivia sat back as she finished her story. Marisol looked out to the empty room and listened to the creeks in the floor. Her hands in her hair, she moved to the cross that was Dylan's and played with it as Olivia was nervous of what Marisol's reaction might be.

"When I came back from visiting Christopher, right after Dylan died, I had a big fight with Mom. She told me how horrible they were to her. I broke this vase that was Sheila's. I felt so horrible about it, so Frannie took me to replace it. I don't know much more than they were horrible to her. Your story makes sense, and now I can piece things together. They were bad to her because she was bad in her previous life. I also do believe what you said. She had God in her heart and it helped her overcome. Things turned around for her when she met Dylan. Then they had a huge challenge right at the beginning of the relationship. But she did believe in him and I must think you are right, she had God in her heart. I believe that is why she stayed with him when times were bad and when they remarried. They both died such a tragic death, but for them to be sick and drawn out would not have worked out for them. They are both a bit dramatic... I mean, seriously. I hope that they are both together in heaven. If this is Sheila and Ashley for my mom and for the hatred to go away, I will be the best mother I can be to them. I will show them the love that Mom gave me. I will break the bad cycle."

They hugged and felt a sisterly bond that I didn't have with mine.

James and Britney, formerly Sheila and Ashley smiled for their morning sleep and molded themselves into their new bodies. They already felt the love.

*   *   *   *   *

Dylan and I fell asleep on the couch. I awoke to him shivering in his sleep and went to grab a blanket for him. Peanut slept soundly in her room. I leaned into Dylan to readjust myself and he was having a dream. He was a bit angry from his facial expressions and had some sweat coming from his forehead. I watched him, confused, as I didn't think that could happen up here. As I was nervous, I woke him, and he was confused as to where he was.

"Dylan, what is wrong. Are you having a nightmare? Does that happen here?" I asked, very confused.

"I am struggling, Valerie. I am fighting with myself to forgive. I just am."

I kissed his cheek and held his hand to lead us up to bed. We went into our perfect cuddle position as we always did, and as I felt my face in the nook of his back, I drifted off.

"Valerie, I still have so much to ask forgiveness for. I still have so many questions for you. I am sure you have them for me too. I know you seem so content. I am struggling with forgiveness. There are things you haven't seen yet, Valerie. It will hurt me, but I understand. Help me to learn to forgive."

I gave Dylan a peck in his nook and grabbed my hand tighter to him. He squeezed me back and drifted into sleep.

The next morning, we all walked to mass. Madeline and Christopher held hands behind us and still giggled like schoolchildren. I held Peanut as I was still absorbing the warmth of her that I wished I had known on Earth. Christopher came beside Dylan and gave him a nod as if he was asking for permission. Dylan nodded back.

"Valerie, James and Britney are beautiful. I bet you are so proud of Marisol."

I looked at him and still did not recognize him.

"I am a very proud grandmother and I am sure that Dylan is a very proud grandfather." I looked straight ahead as I could see them in their cribs looking back up. Dylan and Christopher looked at each other as I still did not process who he was.

"I am so proud of Marisol and hope that they will think of me as one of their grandfathers, Valerie."

I didn't understand what he was saying.

"Well, I am a proud grandfather for sure, Valerie," Christopher said as we walked into the chapel.

I did not process his response. When we came out, Madeline came over to me and asked for all of us to come over for dinner that night. We gladly accepted.

Dylan took Peanut into the house, and as he settled her down, he came over to me and held my hands.

"Valerie, I love you. I want you to know that I love you. No one will break us. Not up here." He gave me a kiss and looked me in my eyes.

"Dylan, I love you too. I agree, we will not be broken when we are up here. I believe that."

"Valerie, do you know who Christopher is?" Dylan asked as he wanted this Band-Aid to be ripped off.

"Madeline's boyfriend? Previous life?"

"Okay, yes. But do you know who he was in our life?"

"I am sorry, Dylan, I don't. What am I missing?"

"*Mi amor*, okay. When you see him, look into his eyes. You will see. Just don't be afraid. Trust in what is in your heart." I was not sure what he was talking about, but I was loving the kisses from him and still so drawn and attracted to him. The distraction took me away from thinking about Christopher and what I didn't see in him, what I didn't remember of him.

We went to dinner and sat on the back deck, and the weather was always perfect each day. The fire in the background, the twinkling lights above us—it was just as I felt it would be. Christopher sat across from me, and Dylan held my hand as we waited for Madeline to join us.

"Valerie, I am also excited to be a grandparent," Christopher said again as he looked at me.

I sat back and did as Dylan told me to do. I looked into Christopher's eyes. I remembered him. I remembered him from a previous life when we were lovers. I was not kind to him either. Then I was gone, but I did love him. I did remember that. I didn't know who I was as that person. It was so foreign to me. I remembered Christopher in our last life, crawling into his bed days before he passed away. I remembered telling him that Marisol was his daughter. I remembered cheating on Dylan and the lies. I was a horrible person. *How did I get to heaven?*

In embarrassment, I excused myself and walked away. I went down the block and into a field that was centered by beautiful flowers. I cried as I didn't understand why I was so lucky to be here. Dylan came around and stood behind me as I didn't know he was there.

"Valerie, it is okay. It is," he said to me as I wept in the garden. He came over to offer me condolences.

"Dylan, I hurt you so bad. I hurt Christopher in a previous life. Why do you both love me so much?"

"Valerie, you have love in your heart. You followed someone you thought you were in love with. You gave us a child when we couldn't have one. I love Marisol and will always think of her as mine. Just as I do about Pri and John. Olivia and Peanut as my paternal children. I love all my kids. Valerie, you are a good person. Forgive who you were. Forgive yourself so we can move on and enjoy our time here. Go and forgive Christopher as he has already forgiven you."

I had a hard time with forgiving myself. I thought I did until I looked into his eyes and saw how bad of a person I was. It was that person I needed to forgive. It took some time. We went back to the dinner table and I looked at Madeline and Christopher as they awaited our return. No questions were asked, and we continued our meal.

Christopher came over to us in the garden. He asked Dylan if it would be okay for us to talk. Dylan made sure I was comfortable, and I then gave the nod that it was.

"Valerie, I know it is so much to learn. It can be overwhelming. I was shocked when I found Madeline and then Sheila. I made foolish mistakes in my life before ours. I shouldn't have run away. I wasted a life. I almost wasted the life I was in with you. I was horrible to my wife, and my daughter didn't want to speak to me anymore. That was painful to go through.

"I remember the life we had, before ours, before I met Madeline. You were not a nice person. You beat me as your slave and drove me to overwork and scared me. I went times without food for the selfishness that you were. I can see it when I look at you. But I can also see you in our past life. The dedication you had to meeting me. The draw of taking care of me—both times, I was down. You gave a daughter and gave me the last moments of my life when you should have let me go.

"I am at peace. I was so in love with Madeline and now I have the time to spend with her and my daughter, Sheila, and that is now our grandchild. It is weird to process, but in another life, you were a product of me. Perhaps that is the cycle of us. Your heart belonged to Dylan, but you had me somewhere in your heart. You brought me back to her. If you didn't, I would still be lost. I am so grateful. I want nothing more than this. Valerie, I want for you to be happy and forgive yourself."

Christopher walked back to the table, and I sat in the light, processing what had just happened. I was so horrible. "Jesus, I want to be forgiven for being such a bad person in a previous life. I don't want that person to ever come back to haunt me or my family." He shined the light brighter and the overwhelming warmth was the answer that I was forgiven. I went back to the table to finish dinner with the family.

"Christopher, I hope that you can forgive me for who I was in a previous life. I was horrible. I hurt you so badly. In this past life, I am grateful that you gave me... us... Marisol. I hope you can forgive me for not exposing it all sooner."

Christopher smiled and leaned into Madeline. She also smiled. "Valerie, everything happened for a reason. I told you already, the past life was a hard one. I have already forgiven you. You gave me a daughter when one of mine would not talk to me. You gave me the most special last days of my life when I thought everyone had given up on me. You brought me to Madeline. I am so grateful. We can all be happy up here in heaven. You and Dylan have Peanut and each other. I, finally, have my time with a daughter I never knew— Sheila—and now I have Madeline. We have it all. So yes, I forgive you. I have love for you and I'm so grateful for all that you have done." He grabbed out for my hand. I gave it to him. and as we squeezed hands. it felt okay to let go of that pain.

*   *   *   *   *

Marisol woke up for a feeding in the middle of the night and took a moment to look at Michael as he was fast asleep. She went in to find Britney crying and James asleep. She held Britney and fed her a bottle as they danced around the room together. She decided to start asking her questions like Olivia was doing.

"So are you Sheila or Ashley? Did you see my momma when you were in heaven? I miss her so much. If you are Sheila or Ashley, I hope that you all had a chance to make up. You are going to have a great life here, Britney, I promise you. I know that you will be loved by us and the whole family. I will make sure you have a wonderful life, Britney, and James too."

With that, she grabbed Marisol's finger and smiled. She knew Olivia was right. It was them. There was peace.

Sheila said to herself, "This is going to be the best life, I know it." She cooed it out, but Marisol understood and snuggled her close before she was ready to drift back off into sleep.

*   *   *   *   *

Dylan and I went to put Peanut to sleep together which was the delight of reading a story and watching her drift into a sound rest.

"Valerie, we have so much to talk about. I know you are still absorbing a lot that goes on up here. It is wonderful to have forgiveness, but we still have some unresolved items to talk about."

"I know, I know. I am so happy that I found forgiveness with Sheila and Ashley. Marisol and Michael will take wonderful care of them. Olivia being there is a great gift. She needs her to rely on. She needs me, and I am not there for her."

"Oh, *mi amor*, don't get upset. She knows you are with her in spirit. You gave her your family as her children. It is the best match."

"Thank you, that makes me feel better." I looked to fall into him for comfort, but he turned away again.

"Valerie, we need to talk. I need to get out of my penance to be able to move on."

"What? I didn't know you were in penance."

"Yes, I have forgiven, Valerie. But there are things that still hurt. Just as Christopher told you in a previous life, I was your child, and you were just as cruel to me as him and others. In our past life, you found me and saved me. I hurt you. I lied to you about Olivia. I had a weak moment when Lydia came to me to tell me that she loved me instead of Miguel. We had sex in the back of the farm. But then she went and ran to Miguel, and suddenly they were getting married. We found out about the baby afterward. I didn't think she was mine. But when I looked at her, I knew. I confronted Lydia several times, and she denied it. John found out one day when he was going through papers and saw her birth certificate. It had my name on it. Lydia and I went back and forth on it and decided to keep it quiet as Miguel

154

and I were in a good place, and she didn't want to mess up the family. It hurt, Valerie, it really hurt. My lies became truths and I forgot them after time.

"Then I met you. You made it all seem so easy and happy. I was finally able to let Lydia go, and she didn't like that. I had chased her for so many years. She knew I still had feelings for her when she married Miguel. I didn't act on it once they were married. She tormented both of us. Her threats were horrible, and when she found out I was with you, she threatened more. Miguel wanted a divorce, we know where that landed him. Pedro was behind it for Matteo and Miguel. So to forgive him to take lives over something we could have worked out really is hard to let go of."

"Dylan, I am so sorry. I know that you blame Pedro for their deaths. I wasn't sure if they were true or not. I know that they are true now. I am sorry that you were tormented by her, by them. But you did forgive, and now we have Peanut. We have each other." I tried again to reach into him for comfort. He pulled away.

"Valerie, there is more. I don't want to forget when I was with Teresa. You pushed me away, Valerie. Your head was somewhere else at night when we slept. I know now that Marisol belongs to Christopher. I know now that you loved me more and it was always me. But then, I didn't. I was so upset, Valerie, I felt like you drove me to Teresa. She dumped me because I cried about you every night. Now, looking at both of our past lives, it is hard to accept. I do love you, I do forgive you. But I think as part of my penance, I need a little bit to process all of this. I hope that you understand."

I stood across from him in the hallway upstairs. The space between us became bigger and bigger. He distanced himself from me. There was so much hurt, I didn't know what to do. I was in heaven and hurt by the man I loved and declared I would love forever. I still love him forever. I nodded my head and started to tear up. I grabbed a bag and packed it. I went in to say goodbye to Peanut.

"Goodbye, my love."

"Mommy, don't leave. It is okay."

"I am going to leave as Dylan is trying to get through his penance. I realize I have to do mine. I love you, Peanut. I am not abandoning you. I am just going to live somewhere else for a while. I want to be over this and move on with you and Dylan."

"Daddy forgives you. So stay. I want you to stay with me."

"Oh, Peanut, I have to leave him be. I will visit you every day, I promise." I gave her a kiss with tears, and she held me close. I left her bedroom to find Dylan sitting at the top of the stairs.

"I hurt you. I understand that. You need time. I love you so much. I want to give you the time you need. I realize this is my penance. On Earth, things were hard. This is probably harder to leave you. I am going to pray for you. I know we will be together again." I went to give him a kiss and he moved his head away. He might have forgiven, but he was not over the hurt. I never wanted to be that person I was in a past life. Never.

I walked, not sure where I was going, and Jesus came outside as I passed the church.

"Valerie, how are you doing?" He stopped me.

"I am sad. I understand I have some penance to do for the mistakes I made. I hurt people in the life before this one. I don't even know who that person is. I don't have the memories. But I want to be with Dylan and Peanut. I really love them with all my heart. I want to do this so we can all be able to move on from here."

"Valerie, you don't have to serve penance for the life you don't remember. You did more good than bad in your past life. This is not your penance. Dylan needs to understand what forgiveness means. He does forgive you. Don't give up on him."

"He pushed me away when I made peace with Christopher. I just want to give him space. I don't want to lose him."

"Then don't. Don't run away from your family, Valerie. If you have me in your heart and them in your heart, it will all be okay. Don't take away the value you gave to so many, including yourself. Remember, there is no judgment here. You are here because I believe in you and love you. You are forgiven. Valerie, don't push me away."

"Oh, I will never push you away. You gave me eternal life. I am so grateful. Please forgive me for not having the right words. I am so grateful and will not turn on you. I am not turning on Dylan, Peanut, or my family. I just want to give him space. I will pray and pray that we can spend the rest of our time together, that he can look at me the way he first did. I need to use this time to figure out how to do that. Is that okay?"

"My child, everything you do is fine. There is no right or wrong. Just don't wait too long. You have been apart for so long. Don't waste any more time."

He gave me a hug and sent me on my way. I found where Frannie lived. She was with Matteo and Albina. They welcomed me with open arms.

"Oh, my girl, how I have missed you!"

Frannie hugged me. I finally got to meet Frannie's husband, Matteo. He was better looking than the pictures. He was tall, like Dylan, dark black hair. I expected him to have gone the same salt and pepper that Dylan did. I could not help but stare at him. He was a replica of Dylan. I know it should be vice-versa, but he looked just like him. Oh, how I was mesmerized all over again.

"Aha! You see the resemblance!" Frannie said as she sat at the table with us.

Matteo insisted we share a tequila. He started the tradition of tequila later in the afternoon on the farm way before my time. Matteo came home from a long day out in the field while Frannie was with the kids doing homework and making dinner. As the sun set, she came out to the porch, he walked up, and they shared that time together. A quick tequila and time alone to talk about the day, the kids. When they started that, they sat with each other to watch the sunset and kissed as he held her tight. Then as time went on, he sat on the opposite side of her. They didn't touch much. She went to be closer to him. He stood up and headed inside. After years, she gave up, stopped meeting him on the porch, and just served dinner at the island.

Here in heaven, they were back to where she remembered the happy times—loving, to be in his arms, to spend the time together they never had that pulled them apart. She had Albina as her friend to share a sisterhood.

"Sorry for staring. Yes, I do see the resemblance. Wow, Matteo, Dylan looks just like you!"

Matteo giggled and was shy as he blushed and turned his head to Frannie for approval to accept the compliment of sorts.

"Dylan was my very handsome son. I am honored that you would say such a thing." He touched my hand and moved back to his drink. We retired to the porch that was our old porch at the farm. It was Matteo and Frannie's house, then Miguel and Lydia, then myself and Dylan, myself and Luke. Now it was John and Clarissa's. It was home. Despite all the places I had lived, it was home.

"Dylan is a tough cookie. He really is. He kept our tradition alive for us. He made it all happen. I watched over all of you. Valerie, thank you for all that you did for my family."

"It was my honor, for sure."

"I know you made amends with Pedro. That is very noble of you. I have learned to forgive him also. It is not easy, but I did. I know you want Dylan to forgive. You have to let him figure it out." Matteo looked out into the farm as we watched Marisol with her babies dancing to keep them from tears. She smiled as this was the best job she was ever given. Michael drove up to the farm and ran out of the car to greet them. He could not finish work fast enough to be with them.

"He wants time away from me. I am just giving him what he needs. I can't ask him again to forgive Pedro. I hope he will find it in his heart. It hurts so much to be away from him."

"Then don't be!" Frannie screamed at me from the other side of the porch. I turned to look at her.

"He won't look at me. He pushed away when I went to kiss him. I left, and he didn't stop me."

"Valerie, you act like you've never met the man. He is a stubborn Latino. Give him a break. Go back to him."

"Can I stay here tonight and think about it? I will see them at mass. I promised Peanut I would see her every day."

"Valerie, of course you can. Stay as long as you need. But don't prolong this. Go and be with him." We cheered glasses as we sat on the farm and admired the family as they settled down for dinner.

*   *   *   *   *

John came back from working on the farm all day and Clarissa waited for him on the porch. She sat with Mary as the sun was about to set and smiled as he came up with his flannel opened and work hat on low to his face.

"Hello, my favorite ladies!" he said as he came in for a kiss. Clarissa grabbed him in for another one, this time a bit longer.

"Mommy!" Mary screamed as she was embarrassed to watch her parents kiss in front of her. They laughed and went in again.

"That was nice. Clarissa, I missed you today." He sat down to feel the sun on his face as it went down. He sat back into the chair and grabbed Clarissa to come in closer.

"It feels nice out here. It feels so calming. Let's eat out here tonight," Clarissa said, and John nodded. He closed his eyes in hope of a quick nap before dinner was ready. Mary came to sit beside him and finished her homework.

I could feel John and came to give him a hug as he was taking his nap. I missed when he was younger and came to cuddle in between Dylan and I as he raced to beat Pri to the spot. "I miss you, Mom," he said in his sleep.

Clarissa opened the door with a tray of food. "John? Who are you talking to?" she said, not realizing that he was asleep.

He quickly picked himself up as he didn't notice how deep he fell. "What? Hmm, I don't know. I fell asleep and I felt my mom. Weird. But it is nice to know she is around us."

Clarissa smiled and hesitated as she went to sit down. John was deep into building his plate, he didn't notice that she was acting awkward. He was just enjoying the day. She went to sit across from John then asked Mary to switch spots with her so she could be closer to him.

"John," she said as she went to sit and snuggle into his arm as he started to eat.

"Yes, Clarissa, my love?" he responded but continued to eat.

She looked at Mary as she did not either get her serious intent to be so close to him at that moment. "I have something for you."

"Oh, yeah? Can it wait until after we eat? I am staving. You sure make chicken cutlets as good as my mom. I don't want them to get cold on me."

She sat back into the chair and ate as well. She might have been annoyed with him, but it was just because she couldn't contain her surprise.

Marisol came over as they were eating and had a moment while the babies were resting.

"Hey, y'all! Just wanted to see if I could go into the attic again? I thought of something I wanted to bring to the house." She was asking for permission as she walked to the door and went inside regardless. They shrugged and continued to eat.

Marisol went upstairs and into the attic. She looked around at all the boxes and found hers from before she went to college. She took out the jar she bought me after she broke Sheila's. She held it close to her and thought of me. She tried to picture me and Sheila together, but realized it didn't matter. She scampered back to her home and waved goodbye as she passed them on the porch. John was used to her always being on a mission and not paying attention to her surroundings.

"What was that about?" Clarissa asked.

John paid no mind. "My sister gets on a mission and she just goes for it. No questions asked. Looks like she went for the jar that she bought Valerie. It was a replacement of something that Valerie had from her mother. She asked me again the other day if I found it. I honestly didn't look. She told me that she and Olivia believed the twins are Sheila and Ashley. She wanted the jar to show them it will stay in the family. It was very special to her. When Valerie died, we couldn't find it. I guess today she remembered where it was."

"What do you have from Valerie that you kept remembering her? I don't think I know of anything." Clarissa asked.

"I do have something. I do. Maybe I shouldn't have been the one to keep it. I was holding it for Pri, but it meant a lot to me. I will show you when we finish dinner."

Clarissa was going through her mind about what it could be, thinking of what he had in his drawers. She could not think of anything.

Marisol ran into the house, so excited to bring the jar to Michael, reminding him they believed Sheila and Ashley were their twins. He laughed at whatever made Marisol happy; it made him happy too.

"Happy wife, happy life," he mumbled as she ran to the sink to rinse it off and fill it with flowers she picked that afternoon on the farm.

"Michael, now we must always keep fresh flowers in this jar on the table. I only want this house to be blessed with happiness and love, Michael. These twins are only going to be filled with love. These flowers will bring us happiness. Keep us smiling. Never let us stop smiling, Michael!" She was very demanding and determined.

Michael was always attracted to her when she acted like this as all he had to do was smile and say, "Yes, dear." He laughed and went back to working on his tablet, listening for the babies to wake up.

*　　*　　*　　*　　*

I went to the empty bedroom at Frannie's and could not sleep. I missed Dylan so much. It was painful. I laid on the bed, staring at the ceiling, and called for him. "Dylan, Dylan…"

No response.

Frannie came into my room and laid next to me on the bed. "He won't respond. You know how he gets when he is confused. He hides. Go back to him, Valerie," she reminded me.

I couldn't move. "Frannie, I want to. But I feel like I need to give him a bit of space. I will decide in the morning."

"You are both stubborn Zavala's. Oh, he misses you, Valerie. He is my son. I know that he does." She came to cuddle with me as I turned myself to the other side. She held me as I fell asleep and could not bear to be alone. She knew it.

The next day, we went to mass and I made my way to Dylan and Peanut. Dylan was cold to me, but Peanut came over to give me a hug. We sat together. Dylan did his best to not show me affection. It was cold. When mass was over, I asked Dylan if he was okay and that I was coming back.

"Valerie, you left. I didn't stop you. If we love each other, we don't leave." He turned and started walking away.

"Dylan, you left me. I never left you. I just gave you a night alone. *One night.* You left me for another woman. I forgave you and took you back. Then you took your life. I can't keep being punished for something you already forgave me for. Dylan! I have told you a thousand times, I want you. No one else. I want you. Let us be a family again. I don't like this. I thought we forgave each other."

He stopped in his tracks then walked back to me. "I did forgive you, Valerie, I did. But you left, I question your love for me. I know you love Peanut. But I question your love for me. I just think maybe you will always be looking for someone better. I know, I should not think like this in heaven. But I saw you talking to Christopher and it just brought back memories. I just... I just... Valerie, this is hard. Maybe it is best if you stay with Frannie for a bit. I need to sort this out. I need to sort this out without you."

With that said, he walked away and left me alone in the street. I went back to Frannie as she heard the whole thing and let me lay in her lap and she caressed my hair.

"I didn't think I could be so upset in heaven. I really didn't."

"Just trust and believe. Don't lose faith, girl, don't lose faith."

I cried the rest of the night and could see him in the bedroom crying himself. *I don't understand why we are in heaven and living apart.* "Dylan, I am never giving up on you. Never. I love you."

*   *   *   *   *

Clarissa brought John into the bedroom after Mary went to sleep. She was so attracted to him in his farm gear and sweat from the day, his tan lines where they cut off at his neck and arms. His face was becoming leathery from the daily sun intake, and not using suntan lotion aged him. To her, he was handsome. He looked like Miguel but acted so much like Dylan. He was very much a product of him.

"Clarissa, feisty tonight. Hold on, hold on. You asked me something and I want to show you."

"John, what did I ask you? It can wait. I want you right now. I really need you." She grabbed at him and started to unbuckle his belt, and as he resisted, he pulled into her and lifted her dress as he could never resist her. He pulled her dress over her head. She kicked off her shoes. She pulled his belt from the loops and threw it across the floor. She took her time to open the zipper and used her feet to move his jeans to the ground. He still worked out daily and held his physique from playing baseball. His boxers were tight and striped loud colors. It made her laugh. She wore a simple bra trimmed in a delicate lace. He quickly tore it off and threw her into the bed. She crawled onto him and finished what she set out to do that evening.

They laid sweaty in the bed and she came to crawl back on him. He screamed out.

"Wait, wait. Hold on. I want to show you something. I want to give you something."

She was confused as she was the one with the news to tell. The excitement was with her, she did not remember what he wanted to give her.

He went into the dresser and opened a tiny jewelry case. It held my wedding band, Dylan's wedding band, and Dylan's cuff links that he wore when he worked in Manhattan. John already wore Dylan's Rolex that I wore when he passed. It suited him. There were some necklaces and jewelry. Mostly the girls have the rest. But in the bottom of that box was the red string ring the girls made for me when we first went to Mexico. It was refurbished for our second wedding. But John kept it. He wanted at that time to give it to Clarissa, to remember his family and the love we held for each other as dysfunctional as it was.

He came to crawl onto her as she held a sheet to cover her middle leaving her legs open. He held her finger to his mouth, then when it was wet, he was able to slip it onto her finger. She was patient as she watched him.

"Clarissa, I love you. I know this looks like nothing, but it is everything to me. I want to keep the family tradition. I want this to be your ring. My sisters made this for Valerie before Dylan and she got engaged. It was our way to say we wanted to be part of the engagement and tell her we wanted her to be part of the family. She loved you, Clarissa. I wanted you to have a big fancy ring, so I gave that to you. But now I want you to know how much I still love you. I feel somehow when I came home, I felt Valerie with me. She wanted you to have this."

She held her hand to her heart and pulled him in for a kiss, and to have him relax onto her. He rested his head against her chest. "John, I love you so much. I just wanted to tell you one thing tonight. You just made it even more special. I know the story of the ring. Olivia told me. I didn't know you had it. But as she was in Mexico, when Dylan gave this to her, she told him something very special. Do you know what that was?"

He looked confused and answered, "She said yes?" Like it shouldn't be a question of what happened.

"No, John. I mean, she did say yes. But most importantly, she told him that she was pregnant."

"Oh, yeah. I guess so. I didn't know until much later in life. But I guess she did." He looked at her to admire her eyes.

"John, are you paying attention?"

"Yes, my love," he said and came in for a kiss.

She stopped his forehead with her hand. "John!"

"Yes?"

"I have been trying to tell you that I am pregnant!"

"What? What? OMG! Really? This is amazing! OMG!" He got up and started to pace around the room, then realized he shouldn't be anywhere else than back with her to admire her glow and kiss her in gratitude. "Clarissa, you have made me the happiest man in the world!"

"John, I love the ring. It means the world to me. I will cherish it as a Zavala family heirloom forever."

"Clarissa! We are having a baby. Oh, I am so happy! I am so happy!" He kissed her and they finished their night in glory celebrating a new life to come.

*   *   *   *   *

Each day we went to mass, and I sat near Dylan as Peanut sat between us. She did her best to get us to touch hands and smile at each other. She was adorable. She grew again since I had been here and was equivalent to about a ten-year-old at this point. I kept staring at Dylan and not asking any further if I could come back. He ran off after mass to avoid me each day. Peanut stayed with me and I walked her back as slow as possible. We got to the door and she asked me each day to come inside, and as I saw Dylan looking from the window with anger in his eyes, I declined.

Madeline came out one day to greet me as I was sad to leave Peanut again. "Valerie, come over and have lunch with us. Don't be sad. He loves you. He does." She held my shoulders and guided me into their home. I was so lost and upset without him.

Christopher gave me a hug as we sat outside and ate lunch. "I don't know what happened. He forgave you. He was so miserable and sad waiting for you to get here. I don't understand why. I try to talk to him and he pushes me away as well. We were in a good place. I don't know what changed in him. I am nervous."

"I am not losing hope, Christopher, I am not giving up on him. I love him so much. I am in heaven and sad. That just shouldn't be. I am afraid it is because he won't forgive Pedro. Do you think that is why?"

Christopher looked at me just as upset for Dylan as I was. "That might be. It is up to God what will be. I will pray for him. That is all we can do right now."

We finished our lunch in silence as if we were mourning a loss. I felt like our family was about to change. I didn't know how to live my life without Dylan. I went to leave, and Madeline grabbed me for a hug. I cried in front of the house. Dylan watched from the front porch and did not get up to console me. When we caught eyes, he was mad. I just walked away. This went on each day. It was really making me so upset. I started to not sit with them anymore. It was a painful way to spend time in heaven. *It shouldn't be like this.*

*   *   *   *   *

The twins turned one and started to walk, which was more work for Marisol to chase after them. Olivia came up to stay with all of them as Clarissa was in her eighth month of pregnancy. John raced to the house each day after he was done with working on the farm. He looked more and more like Dylan every day. The hat, the flannel, how he wore his fancy watch that reminded him of Dylan, of when he was a famous baseball player. He wanted to stay on the farm and be with his family. To keep the Zavala farm alive.

John and Enrique collaborated on their businesses and expanded the name even further. They had locations all around Texas and into Mexico. It kept them in the picture and built the bond between the two locations together. The hatred was gone. It was over.

Enrique and Olivia moved into Sofia's house on the farm and split their time from Mexico to Texas. John and Enrique were as close as brothers. After work, John came running to Clarissa to kiss her, kneeled to kiss her bursting belly, talked to their baby to come, and helped Mary with her homework. Enrique and John shared a beer and tossed around a baseball, discussing business. It was as if they were friends for a lifetime. The twins ran around the front yard, falling after a few steps as they were not confident enough to make it very far. Mary played with them, and when Olivia's kids finished their homework, they ran out to play with them also. Clarissa cooked a big Texas BBQ and had everyone over to sit on the long picnic table that matched Madeline's. They ate as often as possible as a family. There was love. There was laughter. There was conversation that never ended. The night came, and it was hard for them all to want to retire to their own homes.

"You built that, Valerie," Frannie said to me as I watched the loving days they had. It made me cry to not share it with Dylan. I looked back to see him from my view. He watched as he sat on his lawn chair, drinking his beer in the shirt that he hadn't changed for days. He was in his own misery and no one wanted to talk to him anymore. Peanut moved to Madeline and Christopher's and spent days with us at Frannie's house. It was sad. Something was about to change. I was not ready to let go of him. I didn't give up on him. It was as if I didn't believe in God.

The cycle continued, day after day. After mass, we watched the farm and the harmonious lives they had; the twins growing up; Mary being the lucky oldest cousin, taking the job very seriously, directing the other children on the games they should play, taking them on tours of the farm and introducing them to all the animals. Her favorite horse was Mona. They sat in her stall and read to her almost every day. It was very cute. It warmed my heart to watch.

Pri was not doing so well. They went to visit her as often as they could. John felt responsible for her and made more of an effort than the others. They had their own children, and as Luke told me, they did not have the time to care for a child as an adult. She was weak. Her memory was fading. She spent most days in bed. Her boyfriend came to see her and read to her. She looked out the window and watched the animals. I sat with her and played with her hair.

"Thank you, Momma. I want to come and stay with you soon," she said out loud. The nurses took it as a sign that she was losing it talking to me. I was there. Her intuition was strong. Dylan sometimes came and stood behind us. I knew he missed her and missed caring for her. When John visited, she told him the times I came to see her. He always believed her and got upset with the nurses for medicating her during those encounters. He was her protector. He held her and sang to her the way Dylan did.

Yo tengo una guitarra vieja
Preñada con esta canción
Amigos que nunca aconsejan
Y un beso a mi disposición

Lo que tengo es tan poco
Que vale un millón
Yo tengo el aire que respiro
Y el mar to'ito para mi
Amores viejos y suspiros
Y si alguien dice no, yo si
Yo poco que tengo es tan poco
Que es también pa' ti
Las huellas de tus pies descalzos
El humo de la cafetera
Tres cuadros surrealistas falsos
Tu risa que trae primavera
Aun que el tiempo este fatal…

They rocked back and forth. She held his arms tight.

"I am ready to go, John. I want to be with Valerie and Dylan. I miss them. I had a good life. I was well cared for by them, by you. I didn't have to want for anything. But John, I am ready to go. I want to be in heaven and have a life without disabilities. Without people making fun of me. Without people not understanding me. I want to have a life with Valerie and Dylan. I want to be free."

John shed tears as she spoke. He caressed her hair and broke down with her in his arms. "Oh, Pri, I want you to be happy. I want everything for you. I wish you didn't have the disabilities that you have. That held you back. You have so much love in your heart. Your love for the family, your spirituality. Your ability to see Valerie and Dylan when they are with you. I am selfish to want you with me, Pri. I don't want you to go. But I want you to be free, Priscilla. I want you to look for the light and follow it. Listen for Valerie and Dylan. Call for Momma. I won't be mad, Pri. Follow your heart, *mi amor*. Follow your heart. You deserve to be happy."

"John, it is coming. I am going to need to go soon. I can feel that Dylan needs me. I need to be there with him."

John broke down again in her arms. "Go, *mi amor*, go and be with him." He kissed her as hard as he could, and Bingo fell to the ground.

*   *   *   *   *

I sat pews behind the family with Albina, and when mass was finished, Peanut came over as usual. We walked to the park and sat on the swings.

"The twins are beautiful, Valerie. I am so happy for Marisol and Michael. Sheila and Ashley are in good hands.

"They are. I am so grateful that Jesus gave them a chance. Gave me a chance. I think we are all breaking the ugly cycle we were once in lifetimes ago."

"We are, because of you. You helped us. Once upon a time, we all were someone bad. We were all sinners and lost. We had a love for Jesus. He saw it in us and it was within us to love and be loved. It is not that easy for everyone."

"Do you think that Dylan lost faith in love?"

"I do. He forgave, but he lost faith. I pray for him and give him unconditional love. I am not giving up. I believe. Momma, I know you do too. Your faith keeps me going. Your faith gave me what I needed. It all happened for a reason, Mom. I needed to be up here to watch over you. We have this time together now. It will all be okay if you have faith and love in your heart."

"Oh, my wise daughter. I am so grateful for you, *mi amor*." I grabbed her swing to be close to me as I gave her a hug. "Dylan, I am not giving up on you. I believe in you. I believe in us," I chanted out loud.

Jesus came over to Dylan as he walked home from mass in a fog. He was not himself and fading from his being in heaven.

"Dylan, what has happened to you? Why are you so sad? You are upsetting your family and friends. You are pushing Valerie away from you. I placed her in your heart. You are not trusting that love. Why?"

"I am hurt. I forgave her. Now I just don't know. I don't want to be with her. I just..."

"You don't love her anymore, That is upsetting. You forgave, but you do not trust that. You will not forgive Pedro when everyone else has. He is about to go into a deeper level of hell each time you deny him that forgiveness. I don't think you dug deeper into your past lives as once upon a time you were him and Valerie was the one that saved you. Let it go. You grew and learned so much. Why are you going backwards? I am afraid that if you continue down this path, I can no longer have you stay here. It is time to go."

"I don't forgive him. I am not ready to. I am sorry, Jesus, I just need time."

"Time. We don't have that here in heaven. But in hell and on Earth, each second is of value. You can't get them back. I am sad, but I know that you have more good than evil in you, so I forgive you. I will ask you to leave here and I will send you back out there. I can't guarantee that you will go to Earth as your forces from hell also want you. You are letting them get into your head."

Dylan was not understanding that he was letting in evil and it was controlling him. He was not listening to Jesus. He was not seeing that Pedro was trying to replace him, bring him down with him because he was allowing this window to open each time he didn't forgive. It took him further away from Jesus. He was stubborn and not seeing it.

Peanut perked up and she heard the conversation down the street and saw the opening in the ground. Madeline and Christopher came outside. Frannie, Matteo, Albina, Lydia, and Miguel all went over to him as Dylan was now going to take his next step, not knowing where it could take him. Peanut felt upset and saw a fire burning. We looked down and saw Pedro on a large elevator that was about to release deeper down into a fire pit. He looked up at us.

"Valerie, please save me!"

I could see the hurt in his eyes, the forgiveness he was seeking. Peanut screamed, "Do something!"

I grabbed her arm and we ran over to Jesus and Dylan.

"May we all say give peace and forgive Dylan of any ill-will and hurt before he takes on this journey. Dylan, I am with you always, but you must have me in your heart. I am sorry that you must do this as now you have not forgiven, and that is your key to stay here in heaven. So, you must go. I want to tell you…"

"*Wait! Wait!*" Peanut and I screamed as we ran from the park.

Jesus stopped speaking and the all gathered to see us. With panting breath, I stopped and stood across from the open hole and across from Dylan.

"Dylan, Dylan, Dyl, I love you so much. I want us to have a life, have a family here in heaven with no worries, no upset, no drama. I love you so much. I never stopped. I never will. I believe in you. I believe in us. I believe that Jesus gave us this gift. Don't throw it away. Stay, Dylan, stay here with me. With Peanut. Find the love in your heart that Jesus gave you. It is in there. You will be going into hell. You may not get out. Please, take this opportunity to forgive. Look at Pedro, look! He is going in deeper, we can't save him after that. Forgive him. Save him. Give him the life, Dylan, and stay here. I am asking you out of love. I can't lose you, Dylan, I just can't. If you go into hell, it will take me with you, all of us. Stop this cycle here. Let our generations and soul's revivals be able to always come back to heaven. Dylan, you have the power!"

We stopped and looked at him. Pedro looked up, sweating from the fires below him, bruises and ashes on his face, shaking from lack of nourishment, lack of air to breathe, lack of compassion. The elevator slowly lowered. The lights flashed. I looked at Jesus he looked down and held his hand out to him. Pedro held his hand up. "Please forgive me. Please."

"I forgive you, Pedro, I forgive you," Jesus replied. He looked into Dylan's eyes.

Dylan held his bottom lip and brushed his hand through his hair. The moment was tense. I could lose Dylan forever. I could be standing where Pedro was in moments, even though I had Jesus in my heart. I was in Dylan's hands now. "I believe in you, Dylan," I said out loud, confident.

"I forgive you, Pedro, I forgive you," Peanut said and looked at Dylan. The moment was quiet. We sat in silence and watched the elevator move a touch more.

* * * * *

John sat with Pri as she fell asleep. He went to talk to the nurse on call that evening to discuss her condition. "She wants to die. She thinks she is going to die. My sister is not well. Her intuition is always strong. I believe her. Is she that weak?" The nurse looked to the floor as she was not sure how to answer his question.

"She is fading. The doctors are having a hard time to see what it is. We are not sure how long she has. But we are doing everything we can to keep her alive."

John dropped tears and paced with his hands on his side. He held his hat and then moved to his bottom lip. "She doesn't want to live. I completely understand and accept it. She is becoming a vegetable. I'd rather she just go into the sunset comfortably and happy."

"John, we have to take care of the patient and do what is best for her. We can do a no resuscitation order, but right now we need to keep her on the meds."

"I want to take her home and be with me. Can I just discharge her?"

"That is an option. We don't agree with it, but our policy allows you to take her at your will or hers."

"Give me the paperwork. We are going now." He signed papers and they released her from the hospital. He grabbed her things and Bingo from the floor. "Baby sister, I am taking you home."

"Can Bingo come? I am ready to see Valerie. Dylan needs me."

"*Mi amor*, I am taking you home to see them."

"I love you, John."

He placed her in the car where she sank into the seat with her head against the window. He raced to get home. When they arrived at the farm, everyone gathered around as they didn't understand what was happening. He brought her upstairs to her old room where her bed still was, next to the crib they set up for their baby's arrival.

It was next to the window where she could see the farm. She held Bingo and looked outside and felt at peace. She closed her eyes with a smile. She felt at home.

The next few days, she mostly slept and had terrors that woke her. "Dylan, don't go, I am coming, don't do it!"

John and Marisol came to sit by her side to calm her down. Clarissa was days away from birth and was on bed rest. John was torn between the two. Olivia did her best to console and take care of the household.

"Go be with Dylan, Pri," Marisol said holding in tears.

*   *   *   *   *

We gathered around at Madeline's house, setting the long picnic table for dinner. Madeline was grilling steaks, Christopher handed out beers. Peanut set the table. I helped in the kitchen with the coleslaw and chicken cutlets. We sat down and held hands to say grace in gratitude to be in heaven together. The doorbell rang and Madeline went to go answer before dinner was touched.

*　　*　　*　　*　　*

Clarissa screamed out loud as her pains were getting stronger. "All right, this is it, let' go!" He pushed her into the truck and ran upstairs to Marisol and Pri.

"Just go, don't worry, just go," Marisol said to him, holding his arm.

He ran over to Pri, said a prayer to her, and kissed her forehead. He ran to the car and took off to the hospital. As they drove, John said a prayer to Pri and Clarissa.

"Clarissa, I pray that you have a fast, healthy delivery. Pri, I pray that you follow the light and listen for Valerie's voice. Go and be the person you deserve to be with no hurt or disabilities holding you back. Jesus, I pray that you can hear me. I want what is best for Pri. Please let her have the life she deserves in the next one. Her heart is of gold and she always had you in it. I pray for a healthy baby for us that can have the same love she has. I pray!" he cried, holding Clarissa's hand.

She smiled, so proud of him and his bravery.

The baby came quickly. It was a healthy 8.5-pound girl, perfectly pink, and screaming in excitement to be on Earth. She was right away loving and fell asleep in Clarissa's arms.

"Thank you, Jesus, thank you!" John screamed in excitement in the delivery room. They had their special moment together with her and gave her all the love that they could. They were so happy.

"John, what should we name her? What do you think?"

"I know this sounds crazy, but I want to name her Priscilla, after my sister. I can see her in our baby's face. I want this to be her chance at a second life through our baby. I want to give that to her."

"Oh, John, that is beautiful. I love that and agree. Hi, Priscilla, we love you."

Priscilla smiled back, and in her head, she said "Thank you, John. You are giving me the chance to have the life I always wanted. Thank you, John."

*   *   *   *   *

Madeline brought over Pedro who came with flowers, a fresh shower, and shave. He was still and had a light burn on his face as if he had a hard day on the farm. He held out his arm and we all cheered in excitement. He smiled and was starting to relax. He felt good. Christopher went over to give him the first hug, then handed him a well-deserved beer. I sat next to Dylan, curled onto his chest, playing with his cross. I gave him a kiss on his cheek.

We ate dinner and danced to the moonlight. We sat by the fire and watched John and Clarissa enjoy their arrival of Priscilla.

"Cheers to you, Priscilla! We love you and wish you the best life! You deserve it!" Pedro said as he led us in prayer.

"Amen!" Dylan said as he crashed his beer into Pedro's, and they hugged.

When Clarissa and Priscilla went to sleep, we all retired for the night back to the happy harmonious family we were when I came to Texas, when I came to heaven; when I met Dylan and was lifted out from hell; when I found Jesus in my heart.

*   *   *   *   *

Before the dinner, we sat at the window and watched Marisol sitting at Pri's side. Pri slept soundly, then awoke. She sat up and reached out her hand and opened her eyes. She smiled and sank back down into the bed and Bingo fell to the floor. Marisol checked her pulse—she was gone.

Days later, John, Clarissa, and Priscilla pulled up to the farm. The family came around to greet them and welcome the newest Zavala to the family. They were happy. They made their own picnic table for dinner. Mary picked roses from the rose patch to place at the table. On earth the Zavala family prayed for us to watch over them. The Zavala family in heaven prayed to stay in their hearts and watch over them. We all held hands at the same table, in different worlds, and thanked God for the gift he gave us—life, love, and happiness.

CPSIA information can be obtained
at www.ICGtesting.com
Printed in the USA
FSHW012322200319
56467FS

9 781644 583883